Maurice Procter and Th

>>> This title is part of The Murder Room, our series dedicated to making available out-of-print or hard-to-find titles by classic crime writers.

Crime fiction has always held up a mirror to society. The Victorians were fascinated by sensational murder and the emerging science of detection; now we are obsessed with the forensic detail of violent death. And no other genre has so captivated and enthralled readers.

Vast troves of classic crime writing have for a long time been unavailable to all but the most dedicated frequenters of second-hand bookshops. The advent of digital publishing means that we are now able to bring you the backlists of a huge range of titles by classic and contemporary crime writers, some of which have been out of print for decades.

From the genteel amateur private eyes of the Golden Age and the femmes fatales of pulp fiction, to the morally ambiguous hard-boiled detectives of mid twentieth-century America and their descendants who walk our twenty-first century streets, The Murder Room has it all. >>>

The Murder Room
Where Criminal Minds Meet

themurderroom.com

Maurice Procter 1906–1973

Born in Nelson, Lancashire, Maurice Procter attended the local grammar school and ran away to join the army at the age of fifteen. In 1927 he joined the police in Yorkshire and served in the force for nineteen years before his writing was published and he was able to write full-time. He was credited with an ability to write exciting stories while using his experience to create authentic detail. His procedural novels are set in Granchester, a fictional 1950s Manchester, and he is best known for his series characters, Detective Superintendent Philip Hunter and DCI Harry Martineau. Throughout his career, Procter's novels increased in popularity in both the UK and the US, and in 1960 *Hell is a City* was made into a film starring Stanley Baker and Billie Whitelaw. Procter was married to Winifred, and they had one child, Noel.

Philip Hunter

The Chief Inspector's Statement (1951)
   aka *The Pennycross Murders*
I Will Speak Daggers (1956)
   aka *The Ripper*

Chief Inspector Martineau

Hell is a City (1954)
   aka *Somewhere in This City*
The Midnight Plumber (1957)
Man in Ambush (1958)
Killer at Large (1959)

Devil's Due (1960)
The Devil Was Handsome (1961)
A Body to Spare (1962)
Moonlight Flitting (1963)
   aka *The Graveyard Rolls*
Two Men in Twenty (1964)
Homicide Blonde (1965)
   aka *Death has a Shadow*
His Weight in Gold (1966)
Rogue Running (1966)
Exercise Hoodwink (1967)
Hideaway (1968)

Standalone Novels
Each Man's Destiny (1947)
No Proud Chivalry (1947)
The End of the Street (1949)
Hurry the Darkness (1952)
Rich is the Treasure (1952)
   aka *Diamond Wizard*
The Pub Crawler (1956)
Three at the Angel (1958)
The Spearhead Death (1960)
Devil in Moonlight (1962)
The Dog Man (1969)

The Dog Man

Maurice Procter

An Orion book

Copyright © Maurice Procter 1969

The right of Maurice Procter to be identified as the author of this work
has been asserted in accordance with the Copyright, Designs and Patents
Act 1988.

This edition published by
The Orion Publishing Group Ltd
Orion House
5 Upper St Martin's Lane
London WC2H 9EA

An Hachette UK company
A CIP catalogue record for this book is available from the British Library

ISBN 978 1 4719 0259 8

www.orionbooks.co.uk

Prologue

Mrs. Sevenoaks awoke at eight-thirty. She looked at the clock, and at her sleeping husband. She did not have to get up yet. Mrs. Spruce the daily help usually arrived about a quarter to nine and brought up the tea at nine. Her husband never went to work before ten, if he went at all. He was Martin Sevenoaks, the theatrical producer now in television, and she was Amanda Gibbs the rising young actress. There was not an alarm clock in the house.

But the light beyond the curtains was strong. It was a fine morning. A fine morning in April. Amanda slipped out of bed and went to draw back the curtains. She stood looking out at the garden. It looked fresh and dewy in the brilliant sunshine. She did not like this suburban house—she liked *nothing* suburban—but she had to admit that the garden was beginning to look very nice. Those lovely daffodils, she thought. The banners of spring.

So after all it did not always rain in Granchester, she thought with condescension. She was one of those who believed that London was the only city in England, and that Chelsea was the only place in London to live. But Martin had to do this job at the Granchester studios, and this house-and-garden was better than a hotel. It was also better for the dog, Macbeth. He roamed about the garden in the daytime without doing too much damage, though the postman was so much afraid of him that a mailbox had had to be fixed to the front gate. As soon as Mrs. Spruce arrived, Macbeth would be out and about, greeting the day with joyous barks.

Amanda turned away from the window, and at her dressing table she picked up a hand mirror. She examined her face. Not bad for first thing in the morning, she thought, and tried a pout. She had first attracted notice to herself by being able to pose looking like an expensively educated person who had remained completely brainless. She tried the expression, and found that it was still available.

As she put down the mirror she noticed that a drawer of the dressing table had been left some way open. She closed it absently, wondering what Martin had been seeking in there. She looked across at him, and noticed that his watch was not on the low table beside his bed. He had gone to sleep wearing it, she supposed. He had been tired, and he had had a few drinks.

She put on a dressing gown and went downstairs, smiling at the thought that she would have the tea already made when Mrs. Spruce arrived. In the hall, with the door of the big living room standing open, she became aware of the coolness of morning in that centrally heated place. She looked into the room, and saw that one of the windows was wide open. That was not only unusual, it was ominous.

'Mac!' she called. 'Macbeth!'

A sturdy Airedale dog appeared at the window. He loped over the window sill into the room. His honest eyes and wagging stump of tail told her that he was pleased to see her, but it was not his usual boisterous greeting. 'What's the matter with you?' she wanted to know. She went to close the window, but stopped with hands outstretched. A semicircle of glass had been cut away near the catch, and pieces of glass lay on the carpet under the window.

She did not touch the window. Choking with panic she ran upstairs, and the dog followed her. She burst into the bedroom, startling her husband into wakefulness.

'Burglars!' was all she could cry. 'Burglars!'

He sat up in bed and looked from her to the dog. 'Burglars? Never. You're making a mistake.'

Somehow his disbelief calmed her, and she felt safer in his presence. She saw that there was no watch on his wrist. 'All right,' she said. 'Where's your watch?'

He looked at the bedside table. 'I'm damned if I know,' he said.

She remembered the drawer which had been open. In frantic haste she ran to it, and found her jewel case. The case was open, and empty. She threw it down, and burst into tears. 'They took my ring,' she cried. 'And all my lovely things.'

Martin found that hard to believe. There must have been some stupid mistake. Women were always losing their stuff. He demanded: 'How *can* we have had burglars? What was the damned dog doing? He never made a sound.'

She was still weeping bitterly, but she managed to say: 'Go and look downstairs.'

He went at once. The dog went with him, and returned with him. 'Yes,' he agreed. 'We've been done. They didn't touch the safe, but they got the money I'd left in my study. And my watch, of course. They must actually have been in this room. The nerve of it!'

He turned reproachfully to the dog. 'Macbeth,' he

said. 'You let us down completely. I've a good mind to give you the hiding of your life.'

Macbeth wagged his tail, and looked apologetic. 'He doesn't know what you mean,' Amanda said. 'It's only because you're being stern with him.'

Martin still regarded the dog. 'I don't understand it at all,' he said. 'He's always as keen as mustard.'

'Perhaps they drugged him, somehow.'

'How? Normally he would have raised all hell before they could get the gate open. You know what he's like. "Macbeth does murder sleep." '

He went to the wardrobe, and found his wallet had been taken. His diamond cuff-links had been taken too.

'Ah well,' he sighed. 'I'd better call the police.'

The police came promptly: two C.I.D. officers. Macbeth dived through the open window and went roaring down to the gate when he heard their car stop outside it. They had to wait there until Martin came to hold the dog, who was so determined to tear those two detectives to pieces that he had to be chained. Mr. and Mrs. Sevenoaks said that this was normal, so that they could not understand about the burglars. They told the officers so. The two men smiled ruefully. They had met this situation before.

1

It was, of course, the Dog Man again.

'It has me beat,' said Detective Sergeant Devery, as he drove the C.I.D. car back to Headquarters. 'Airedales, Alsatians, Collies, Corgis, Poodles and Poms. They're all the same. Not a murmur.'

Detective Constable Cassidy was in the passenger seat. He glanced sidelong at the sergeant. Casually intent on his driving, that young man looked really handsome in profile. It had been said, years ago, that he was too handsome to make a good policeman, but that verdict had been proved to be wrong. Cassidy, a powerful, snub-nosed Irishman, respected him, and envied neither his good looks nor his rank. Cassidy was older, and he could have been a sergeant years ago if he had wanted to bother his head with the examinations. He took orders from Devery, and was content with a sly dig now and again. He liked to prod the English, and he often had an airy Irish answer to an English problem.

'It must be the fairies,' he said now, with sarcasm.

'Ah,' said Devery, mocking his accent. 'Would it be the leprecorns and the banshees, now?'

'Or it could be the gypsies,' said Cassidy, more seriously. 'You remember Gabriel Lavengro? He could charm the birds from the trees, and we saw him charm a horse. Why not a dog?'

'Gabriel Lavengro failed to charm the hangman,' said Devery shortly.

'And his brother, Lucifer?'

'Shut up tight. As mad as a March hare. I checked on it days ago.'

'Ah, you thought of gypsies, then?'

'Naturally. And of every other type who might have a knack of quietening strange dogs. He must have an aura, or a certain smell. Whatever it is, it acts like magic. The dog gets it before it hears him coming, and it doesn't even make a preliminary growl.'

'But he's no peterman. He hasn't touched a safe yet. He doesn't get all he can out of his jobs.'

'All right, call him a brilliant amateur, or a clever mug. He doesn't need to open safes at the rate he's going. Added up, he's got away with ten thousand quid's worth of watches and jewelry, and more than a thousand in cash. Look what he got in this morning's effort. The Guv'nor'll go scatty when he hears of it.'

Cassidy thought about that. He also reflected that he was the subordinate here.

'*You'll* have to tell him, Sergeant,' he said smugly.

Devery grinned. 'We'll do it together, Cassidy. I might want to stand behind you.'

Detective Chief Inspector Martineau was the head of A Division C.I.D., and he merely sighed when Devery went into his office and gave him the news.

'Have you got any ideas yet?' he asked.

'None that are any good. I've made every possible inquiry.'

'So have I. And I've read everything I could find.'

Devery nodded. Aniseed had been talked of, and liver both raw and cooked. Martineau had tried these so-called pacifiers in attempts to approach the canine guardians of houses which had been burgled. None of them had soothed the savage breast. One dog had succeeded in biting his leg, and another had torn his trousers. All the animals at the raided houses had been males, and the possibility of using a bitch in season had been suggested. Martineau had asked around, and was waiting for the time when someone would be able to let him use such an animal.

As a matter of routine, several of the police dog handlers were instructed to approach Macbeth separately on his own ground. It was no use. He threatened all of them, and would undoubtedly have attacked them had he been free to do so. That was one more indication that the elusive Dog Man was not just a man who understood dogs and did not fear them. It seemed certain that, if he did not use a bitch, he must have some very special and secret charm for dogs.

Martineau discussed the matter, not for the first time, with Sergeant Hildred, the officer in charge of the Granchester City Police dog squad. He remarked: 'I'm wondering what would happen if the Dog Man came up against a highly intelligent and specially trained animal, like one of our own.'

Said Hildred grimly: 'I only hope I'm there when he meets one of *my* dogs in the right circumstances. I'd love to see him try it on with Saracen. That old character don't charm so easy.'

'He might meet a dog like that, one night,' Martineau said hopefully.

Hildred needed only the slightest excuse to talk about dogs. He said: 'There could be a psychological angle.'

'Ah, yes. I remember reading about a scientist who trained a lot of dogs and then got them all confused by doing things a bit different. Now who was it? A Russian sort of a name.'

'Pavlov, or summat like that,' said Hildred, brushing the remark aside. 'I've seen an intelligent dog beaten by psychology, where a stupid mutt wouldn't have took any notice. You may remember I used to be in the Riding.'

Martineau nodded. Hildred had transferred from the West Riding Police to Granchester City for the sake of his peace of mind. His wife had wanted to be near her mother, in the town where she had been born and raised.

Hildred continued: 'Up in the dales I've had as many as a hundred farms on my beat. The dogs were border Collies, black and white usually. The farmers used to call 'em "pure bred curs". They were first-class working dogs, and some of 'em were so clever it was uncanny. But a lot of 'em didn't see a stranger once a month, and, Boy, were they savage? But if you had to go up to a farm to look at some pigs on licence, well, you had to go. I've had some rough times with farm dogs. The only way I kept 'em off was by pointing my stick. If they got hold of the end of the stick I could lay my feet into 'em, but most of 'em were too canny for that. I remember once I was having a real harassing time with one of 'em, and the farmer came out to see what the commotion was about. He leaned on the gate and had a good laugh before he called the dog off. Then he told me: "Tha just wants to tell it to come to thee. That's all tha needs to do wi' a good dog." '

'And did it work?'

Hildred was not going to let the interruption ruin his story. He went on: 'I didn't think much of his idea, but I tried it a week or two after. A farm dog came at me showing more teeth nor a crocodile, so I said to it: "Come 'ere." Not soft like, but real loud and bossy. Well, it stopped snarling. It put its tail under its backside and went back about ten yards, and stood looking at me. When I went up to the farm it followed me, barking, but it kept its distance. All the time I was at the farm, it wouldn't come near me. This farmer wasn't as dog-wise as the other one. He said: "Did yer manage to reach it wi' yer stick?" I said: "I never touched it," but he wouldn't believe me. He said: "Yer must a-done." '

'Did the trick always work?'

'About four times out of five, and that saved me a right lot of trouble. A real bit of psychology, it was.'

'You confused the dog by speaking to him as if you owned him. That made him stay at a safe distance. But he did bark at you.'

'Yes. But he was proper flabbergasted. That's because he was brainy. I couldn't have confused a dog that was stupid enough to be confused already.'

'How do you think one of your police Alsatians would react to the sort of command that was given to the sheepdog?'

Hildred pondered, and shook his head. 'I don't think it would work with one of mine. They're too well-trained. When I train my dogs I think they gradually realise there's a reason for everything. I never risk spoiling 'em by acting unreasonable.'

'But that's your very argument against the sheepdog. Your own dogs might react the same way to a stranger who spoke out of order.'

Hildred considered that, and decided to scrub round it. He said: 'Of course any animal can be frightened by summat real strange. I've heard of a fellow scaring off a real savage dog by getting down on his hands and knees and roaring like a lion. I've heard of it, but I wouldn't like to try it.'

Martineau looked at the sergeant, and reflected on the old belief about people who lived with dogs. With his long lip, heavy jowl, flat cheeks, and brown eyes earnestly asking to be taken seriously, Hildred did indeed look a little bit like a Great Dane.

The C.I.D. man succeeded in looking suitably serious. 'I don't know, Sergeant,' he said judiciously. 'With your knowledge of dogs, you might be the very man to get away with a stunt like that.'

9

2

The Dog Man burglaries continued, with no clues for the baffled police to work on. The jobs occurred on fine nights, about twice a week, and always at a house where a dog was kept. It was thought that the thief chose such houses because he was not at all worried about the dog, and because people who kept dogs would sleep more soundly because they felt more secure. Meanwhile the police did what they could. They made every effort to trace the stolen jewelry. Officers on night duty were specially alert. Informers were promised good money for information. But no information came. The narks, snouts, and noses were as baffled as the police.

But about three weeks after the Sevenoaks robbery, there was a break in the pattern. There was a suburban burglary which had all the signs of a Dog Man job, but the dog was missing as well.

'This could be it,' said Sergeant Hildred with a certain amount of jubilation. 'I thought it might happen eventually. The dog has followed the burglar home.'

The dog was a white miniature poodle, and the woman who owned it was more concerned about it than she was about her missing jewels. Photographs of the little animal were available, studio size, mounted and framed. The name was Poppet, and Poppet had never before wandered from home in all the three years of his sheltered life. Photographs were reproduced and issued to all ranks of the force, and to stations of the County police and other neighbouring forces. Also, without delay, the County's bloodhounds were borrowed. Poppet did not have a kennel, he had a smart, quilted basket in the house. The hounds sniffed at the basket, then trailed round and round the suburban garden. Eventually, on a little embanked shrubbery, they found the place where Poppet had gone over the garden wall.

They followed a trail which had been broken and overlaid by traffic, human footfalls, and other dogs, but miraculously it seemed they did not lose the scent. Fortunately the trail did not go into the city, but outward towards the countryside to the east. Eventually all houses were left behind, and the trackers were at the edge of the moors. Here it seemed that Poppet had really enjoyed his outing. Following his tracks the hounds led their handler over low walls, in and out of rough fields, and under culverts. Then suddenly all that nonsense ceased. The bloodhounds raised their heads, wagged their tails, and made a beeline for open country. Their handler was disgusted. He said: 'I think they've scented a bitch in season.'

Sergeant Hildred was acting as helper. 'Never mind,' he said. 'The poodle might have scented it as well. Let's keep going.'

The hounds pulled hard up the gentle slope of a low hill. The road which they had left ran round the hill. In the car which had been following, Detective Sergeant Devery and Detective Constable Hearn went ahead along the road.

The low hill was much steeper on the other side. At the top of it, the County handler checked the hounds and stood at gaze. Down below, near the road again, was a sort of encampment. There were two quite large, low-slung trailer caravans, with a Land Rover standing near them. The vehicles were grouped in the corner of a rough field with broken drystone walls, and obviously the field had been allowed to revert to moorland. But outside the gateless gateway of the field there was a wide border of fairly good pasture beside the road. Along this border, five ponies were tethered at intervals. A stout woman was hanging washing on a line strung between the two caravans, and two or three children were playing around there. Near the gateway, half a dozen dogs were hanging about. The smallest dog was noticeably white.

'There he is, the little rascal,' said Hildred. 'Among the gypsies, by God!'

As the two men watched, the police car came along the road and stopped at the encampment. The County man grinned, and said: 'Your C.I.D. has beaten you to it.'

'They're good at that,' Hildred growled. 'We'd better not go down there with these hounds. No point in letting those folk know we've had bloodhounds on the job. Suppose you take 'em back down to the road, and we'll pick you up with the car in a few minutes? I'll go and see what goes on with the gypsies, if that's what they are.'

The County man turned back with two reluctant hounds, and Hildred went on down to the encampment. When he arrived there he saw that Hearn was holding the white poodle on a dog lead made from a piece of string. The other dogs were two sheepdogs and three obvious mongrels. They waited quietly, with a rather pathetic air of hopefulness. Two dirty little boys and an equally dirty little girl stood staring at Devery and Hearn. As Hildred joined them the stout woman finished her pegging out, and retired to one of the caravans. At the door she turned and spoke curtly to

12

the children. They obeyed her at once, and moved away.

The C.I.D. men were also joined by a stocky, swarthy man in breeches, gaiters, and an old sweater. This man seemed to know at once that he was dealing with detectives, but he was unconcerned about it. He remarked: 'Found your dog, have you?'

'It's a very valuable dog,' Devery told him.

The man was good-naturedly contemptuous. 'Some woman's darling,' he said. 'You couldn't rightly call it a dog.'

'How long have you had him?'

'Now you can't say as I have had him,' the gypsy retorted. 'No more than I've had these other odds and sods.' He pointed to where a big lurcher glowered from beneath his caravan. 'They've all come here after that bitch,' he said. 'I haven't made up my mind yet whether I want her lined. That big sheepdog don't look so bad. I might let him have a go.'

Devery looked at the tiny white poodle and grinned. 'Your bitch looks as if it could eat this one for breakfast.'

'With a bit of bacon rind,' the gypsy agreed without a smile.

'How long are you likely to be here?'

'Well, summer's coming on. We might stay till the back end of the year. I've got some nice Galloways to sell. There'll be a fair or two, I expect. You'll notice we're not camped at the roadside, and we have permission to be on this ground. There's nice clear water in the brook there, and we're not polluting it. We have chemical closets, and there's a proper ditch by the road. We're no bother to nobody.'

'Apart from horse trading, what will you do for a living?'

'Oh, I might get a job of some sort. And I'm manager of an act. It should go well in Granchester. Two Spanish dancers, with a guitar. They have to have a manager 'cause they don't know much English. They live in the other caravan. Brother and sister, and their father plays the guitar. He's damn good at it, too. He makes some of these pop-group guitarists look like amachoors.'

The policemen looked at the second caravan, and saw a girl come to the door and shake a duster. They thought she looked typically Spanish, and in fact she was the Spanish physical ideal. She was of medium height and beautifully shaped. Her face was not at all aquiline, having a straight nose and a firm round chin. She had a warm, brownish skin and roses in her cheeks, and her hair was black and lustrous. In movement she was brisk but graceful. Even the homely action of shaking a duster was attractive.

The three policemen stared. No doubt the girl had seen them, but her lovely brown eyes gave no hint that she had. Her glance did not linger at all. Had they but known it, that also was typical of Spain, where a respectable girl will always ignore the existence of a strange man.

When she had gone back into the caravan, Devery asked: 'Is that the dancer?'

'That's her. I met her father when they were with Singleton's Circus, doing their act. I was a horse trainer. The circus went bust, and the stock was sold off. That's how we got these caravans and ponies.'

'How did the Spaniards like the English winter?'

'They didn't, but they're tougher than you'd think. Anyway they had their work permits and they decided to stay on and see how they made out. They're gypsies, you know. *Gitanos*, they call 'em in Spain.

"Gitano" simply means "Dancer", they tell me.'

'So in Spain all gypsies are called dancers?'

'That seems to be it. Anything else you'd like to know?'

'Just your name, for the report about the dog.'

'Smith. Jesse Smith. My father was Jesse and so was my grandad.'

'All right, Jesse. Thanks for the information. We'll be on our way.'

'Will you be coming back?'

Devery shrugged. 'Somebody might want to know something more about this poodle.'

'Well, nobody here ever touched it. We didn't feed it and we didn't fasten it up. Nobody can say we were keeping it.'

'No? Well, it all depends on the bosses. Cheerio.'

The three policemen went and got into the car. After a final regretful look at the big lurcher, Poppet also hopped in and made himself comfortable across Hearn's thighs. Devery drove back to where the bloodhounds waited with their handler. Poppet yapped boldly at the hounds. Stolid and melancholy now, they gazed at him without interest.

There was a conference. Devery was aware that he was operating in the County Police District. That was why his talk with Jesse Smith had been more like a friendly chat than an interrogation. He would have to go back to town and report, so that any further action could be taken with proper County co-operation. But he did not want to leave the gypsies entirely unobserved. It was finally decided that Hearn should go up to the top of the hill and watch the encampment from there.

'See if they do anything out of the ordinary,' Devery

advised. 'I'll see that you get a relief in an hour or two.'

In the C.I.D. office at Headquarters, Martineau scratched Poppet's head while he listened to Devery's story.

He commented: 'That gypsy knows his onions, putting his caravans through that gateway. Under the Highways Act, 1959, our gracious and big-hearted government denied the gypsies certain rights of movement and residence. They are not allowed to camp at the roadside or on common land. Only holidaymakers and suchlike people are allowed to do that. The freedom of the roads is not for the poor gypsy. How's that for racial tolerance?'

Devery had no observations to make about racial tolerance, so Martineau went on: 'I'll get in touch with the County. We'll go up there with a warrant and search those caravans.'

The matter was arranged, and the search was made. Nothing significant was found in the caravans, not even a glass cutter. Rings worn by Mrs. Jesse Smith and the Spanish girl did not correspond with the description of any of the rings on Martineau's list of stolen jewelry, and neither did either of the watches worn by the Spanish father and son.

Mrs. Smith, stout for a gypsy but nevertheless of a gypsy appearance, was laconic and resentful when questioned. Martineau doubted if she had any information to give, but he became certain that if she had, she was not going to give it.

The Spanish girl's name was Concepcion, called Conchita, and her surname was Segura. All the detectives there thought that she was very beautiful and terribly haughty. Cassidy, a brave man, tried her with a few quips out of Martineau's hearing, but her chill indifference withered his cheery mood.

'Jesus,' he confided to the grinning Hearn. 'I didn't know they had icebergs in Spain.'

The Spanish father, Salvador Segura, was a quiet, courteous man whose manner nevertheless suggested that it would be unwise to offend him. He was lean and compact, not very tall but certainly not physically negligible. It was perhaps just as well that he had not heard Cassidy trying to get on terms with his daughter.

Salvador's son Jose, called Pepe, was in his early twenties, and in a physical sense was a smaller model of his father. He was darkly handsome. He tried to be dignified and succeeded in being surly. Father and son were interrogated briefly. They had not much English, and the police had less Spanish, and Jesse Smith was a very poor interpreter. The girl Conchita was not interrogated at all, because when spoken to she calmly failed to answer.

The search did not seem to worry the Spaniards, and perhaps they thought that it was the merest routine for British police officers to search gypsies. But Jesse Smith appeared to be perturbed. Martineau explained to him that the white poodle's departure from home was connected with a robbery there.

'A burglary, was it?' Smith said. 'Well, you'll find no evidence around here.'

'You'll admit it's a bit odd, that little dog finding his way right out here.'

'They'll go a long way after a bitch. It's surprising how they get the scent.'

'Right through the scent of petrol fumes, people, and other dogs?'

'It was in the middle of the night, wasn't it? The air

is cleaner at night. They can follow the scent a lot easier.'

Not quite satisfied, Martineau ended the talk and withdrew his men. Sitting with him in his car, Devery remarked: 'When we came up here earlier today, the bloodhounds were very interested in a culvert down here. They fairly sniffed around. It occurs to me that we might have a good look ourselves.'

'Show me,' said the chief inspector.

They stopped at a place where the secondary road crossed a tiny moorland stream. The little bridge which had been made there was an arch of solid masonry, probably erected when the road was little more than a pack-horse trail. The two detectives climbed down, and inspected with their flashlights.

'They built really well in those days,' Martineau commented. 'I expect all this mortar is rotten, but the stones fit so closely they can't collapse.'

'Good stone,' said Devery. 'Millstone grit.'

One particular stone caught Martineau's eye because there was no moss in the joints between that stone and its neighbours. He took out his knife and dug into the 'mortar'. The blade went in easily. He dug some of the 'mortar' out and smelled at it. He rolled the soft stuff between finger and thumb.

'A child's modelling clay,' he said. 'We might find something here.'

He began to scrape out clay, and Devery hurried away for tools. He returned with a screwdriver and a tyre lever. Eventually they were able to ease out the stone. The cavity behind it was deeper than might have been expected. Martineau reached in and pulled out a canvas bag. His flashlight revealed that there was nothing else in the hole.

Outside the culvert, in the light of day, the two policemen peered at the glittering contents of the bag.

'Here's our jewelry, I think,' said Martineau.

'It looks as if we might have got all of it.'

'Yes.' The D.C.I. held up the bag and studied its shape. 'Do you know what I think this is?'

'*I* think it's a horse's nosebag.'

'And *I* think you're right,' said Martineau.

3

When examined and identified, the jewelry in the nosebag was found to be loot from the Dog Man jobs; almost all the rings, brooches and watches which the man had stolen in Granchester. This 'turn-up for the book' eased matters considerably in the C.I.D. It was Stolen Property Recovered, the statistics of which invariably showed a much lower average than Crimes Cleared.

The finding of the jewelry naturally increased the police suspicions of the Jesse Smith-Segura set-up, but the encampment was in the County Police District, and so was the culvert to which the thief was expected to return. The County were asked to give the matter their attention, and this they promised to do. But the County's involvement was not so urgent as the City's, and this led the City to feel that there might be a certain lack of vigilance.

'Well,' Martineau commented. 'We can't keep nattering at another force. We'll just have to do the best we can for ourselves.'

The Granchester police set up an observation post

near their boundary on the way from the encampment to the city, so that from there they might be able to follow any Smith or Segura and ascertain his business in the town. But these observations were not very satisfactory, because the road from the moors was tributary to a busy main road. Even in the small hours of the morning there was a considerable amount of traffic. Still, as Devery remarked, there were not too many Land Rovers about in the middle of the night.

But the Dog Man burglaries did not cease, though the County observers reported nothing unusual and nobody went near to the culvert where the jewelry had been hidden. Then it became evident that Jesse Smith had justified himself as manager of the Segura song-and-dance act. The trio appeared at the Tahiti Club in Granchester. Moreover, they continued to appear, and they became a popular feature of the floor show. In the line of duty Sergeant Devery went to see their act, and he was impressed. Salvador was more than merely competent with a guitar, and both dancing and singing were good. Watching Conchita in a solo dance, Devery realised that there was indeed a technique in the use of the castanets. With admirable restraint the girl kept her fingers still until the dance attained a crescendo of music and movement, and then the castanets began an unexpected rattle which was actually thrilling. Also, brother and sister danced well together, and they sang together with an exquisite harmony which sounded so easy and natural that it seemed to be quite unpracticed. The girl's voice was strong and full, and sometimes it seemed to be deeper than her brother's. Devery became convinced that the Segura family at least had no need to steal for a living.

Always the Land Rover was tracked from the city

boundary to the Tahiti Club. It always went directly there, and late at night it went straight home from there, and it did not stop on the way. But the burglaries continued. It seemed to Martineau that half the dogs in the town would be in disgrace.

April drew to a close, and of course the nights became shorter. In another month's time there would not be much more than three hours of darkness in fine weather. Those hours would be the Dog Man's. Between midnight and two in the morning seemed to be his time. He could continue his criminal career all through the summer, unless it was a very wet one. The police had noticed that he only operated in dry weather.

The weather stayed fine for him. But it was also fine for the police, and there was no great worry about him except in the C.I.D. and among the higher ranks. For the uniform ranks even beat duty can be tolerable on a fine night in May, and in the suburban and semi-rural outskirts of a city it can be quite enjoyable. One such beat was the area around Kingsmead, east by southeast of the city centre. The constable who policed it on Nights for the first fortnight in May was called Baines. The beat was generally thought to be 'a doddle'. Baines thought so too, but there was one night during those two weeks which he was never to forget.

The night was a Wednesday, and it was still and moonlit. At one o'clock, riding a motor-cycle, P.C. Baines burbled quietly into the tiny hamlet of Kingsmead. There, by the public telephone box, was his one o'clock conference point, where his sergeant or inspector could pay him a routine visit if that should be necessary. He stopped his engine and sat astride his machine, listening to the night. Dead quiet, he thought.

Not a rustle from the trees, not even the sound of a distant car. He reflected that this peaceful spot, lately taken over by the growing city, would be ruined when the tall blocks of flats started to go up. Lovely, it was. Just the little old church, the vicarage, the village inn, the post-office-and-general store, the three rows of cottages, and nothing more. Perfect, it was.

The air was heavy with the scent of hawthorn blossom, and there was a lighter, sweeter scent which made him wonder if the honeysuckle was in flower. Still marvelling at the sweetness, he took off his peaked cap and from it he extracted a half-smoked cigarette. Still listening intently, he smoked the cigarette down to a stub. He heard nothing, and saw no movement. Not even a cat was stirring.

He dismounted, and went to 'try-up' the inn and the post office. By the light of the illuminated telephone box he looked at his wrist-watch then he returned to his machine and made a radio contact with Headquarters.

'All quiet here,' said the radio clerk, as he booked the contact.

'All the world is asleep out here,' Baines told him, knowing that the answer would be a smile.

He started his machine and rode three hundred yards to the actual boundary of the city, as he was required to do. There the road entered a wood, and it was made shady by big beech trees on both sides of the boundary. He pottered along in second gear at only about ten miles an hour, being in no hurry and not wishing to rouse all Kingsmead. As he made a neat U-turn at the boundary his eye caught a flicker of movement under the roadside trees. Instantly he switched his twin headlights from dim to full, and pointed his

motor-cycle at the place where he had seen movement.
There was nothing.

But Baines had seen something. A large animal or
a man, he thought. Moreover, he was sure that the
movement had been furtive. Somebody or something
wished to avoid him. He turned off the road. There
was no ditch on that side of the road, and he could ride
in and out among the trees. He found nothing.

Beyond the narrow belt of trees was a tall, strong
hedge. He stopped beside the hedge and listened. There
was no sound. He assumed that no creature larger
than a fox could go through the hedge without making
a noise. Was there a gate, then? He dismounted, locked
the steering of the motor-cycle, and went looking for
a gate in the hedge. He found one eventually, but it
was well beyond the city limits. The hedge bounded
the wood on that side, and a little sandy lane started
at the gate and went through the wood to the road.

Baines leaned on the gate and looked at moonlit
pasture land. He clearly saw the forms of cattle, resting
and ruminating. Nothing had disturbed them, at any
rate. He returned to his machine, a puzzled man. He
felt sure that he had seen something higher at the shoulder than a dog, and it had fled at great speed and very
quietly. Its evasive action had been such that he had
not seen which way it went among the trees. A pony
or a cow? No. Too quick and quiet. One of the Kingsmead Hall deer? Possibly, but hardly likely. Some
sort of a bird? That was it, probably. A big owl flying
under the trees. Owls were silent in flight. Yes, it must
have been an owl. All that bother for a bloody owl.

Once more on his motor-cycle, Baines returned to
the village. He had one more task before he went on
his way. He rode his machine through a handsome

stone archway near the church, and thus entered the Kingsmead Hall estate. There was no gate. That was further up the drive, at the Hall itself. The drive was of smooth tarmac with low, white, single-bar fences on each side. These were the fences of the cricket field and the football field which Sir Richard Falcon had given to the village. When the fences ended the drive ran across open parkland, but not for a great distance. In a minute or so Baines stopped his machine at the gates of the Hall itself. The gates were closed. Had they been open, the P.C. would have turned round and ridden away at speed. He had never been beyond those gates, and for a very good reason.

The reason was the dog which ran loose inside the walled grounds at night. It was a Dobermann of terrifying size and disposition, and nobody took chances with it. During the day it was kept under close control, and when some member of the household took it for a walk it was always muzzled. Its name was Rajah.

Baines dismounted at the gate. He expected to see the dog, and when it did not appear he went and looked through the wrought ironwork. He looked to left and right of the drive, and discerned Rajah lying in wait in the shadow of a rhododendron.

'Hello there, Rajah,' he called softly. 'You won't catch me that way.'

In the shadow there was a faint glimpse of white as the dog bared his teeth.

'Aren't you coming to be stroked, then?' asked Baines, who would not have ventured to put his hand within snapping distance.

Rajah came to the gate. He glared at the policeman with luminous yellow eyes, and growled his hatred.

Baines liked all dogs, though he did not trust all of them. He admired Rajah, because he was a fine animal; a beautiful animal really, when he was not showing hostility. Baines would have liked to be friends with him, though he still would not have trusted him entirely. Rajah was a foreign sort of dog, he believed. Dobermann Pinscher, wasn't it? A sort of German. He presumed that German dogs would be different from English dogs, just as Germans were different from Englishmen. Their minds would work in a German sort of way, and therefore they could never be thoroughly understood, and therefore not completely trusted. That was what Baines thought.

'*Achtung!*' he said, though not loudly. 'All well up at the house, is it? You little pet, you. You bloody great man-eater.'

Rajah did not growl. He leaped suddenly at the gate, shaking it with the impact of his forepaws. Involuntarily, Baines stepped back a pace.

'Oh, all right,' he said in disgust. 'Stay by your miserable self, and be damned to you.'

He returned to his motor-cycle, and rode back to Kingsmead. He did not see the lurking figure which had been waiting for him to go, a figure which now moved silently across the parkland towards the gate where Rajah waited.

Before he left Kingsmead Baines went once more to the boundary, but he saw nothing which moved. He sat on his machine for five minutes, listening. He heard nothing except the hoot of an owl.

'Yes, it must have been an owl,' he decided, as he started his motor-cycle. As he passed through Kingsmead again he saw a big car come from the direction of Granchester and turn to go through the estate archway. It looked like Sir Richard Falcon's Rolls-Royce, with Sir Richard driving.

'Coming home late from some do,' Baines surmised. 'I hope his dog doesn't bite him.'

At two o'clock he had a conference point a mile and a half away. As he sat listening to the night's silence he heard the distant howling of a dog. It was a sad, sad cry.

'Somebody dead?' he wondered. 'Happen it's Rajah howling. Happen Sir Richard has give him a damn good kick.'

4

Detective Chief Inspector (D.C.I.) Martineau walked into A Division Headquarters at precisely nine o'clock the next morning. On his way to the C.I.D. main office he noticed that Detective Chief Superintendent Clay's office door stood wide open. As he passed the doorway he saw Clay sitting at his desk. 'Morning, sir,' he said, without stopping.

'Martineau,' Clay said. 'I want you.'

The D.C.I. went into the office, and was told to shut the door. He closed it, and then sat down on one of the visitors' chairs.

'Tired already?' Clay asked drily.

'No, sir.'

'Well, I am. I was got out of bed in the middle of the night.'

Clay was chief of the Granchester City C.I.D., responsible for the detective work in all its divisions. So, Martineau thought, it's a big job. But he remained silent, and waited for information.

Said Clay: 'Sir Richard Falcon was murdered some-time around half-past one.'

Martineau had been lounging. He sat bolt upright. His hard, not unhandsome face reflected his surprise, then almost at once his grey eyes narrowed in con-jecture.

'Where?' he asked.

'At his home.'

'That's D Div.'

'Yes. And D Div. is short of a D.C.I. at the moment.'

'Is Chief Inspector Naylor poorly?'

'I don't think he's feeling too good at the moment. He was attacked by a savage dog. It ripped his arm and tore his hand, then went for his head and laid his face open. It bit three more men too, but they managed to get it off Naylor and hold it down till somebody came.'

'Whose dog was it?'

'Sir Richard's. One of those big smooth-haired dogs with a long foreign name. A sort of a hound of the Baskervilles. Half Great Dane and half black panther, I shouldn't wonder. Anyway, it's a fearsome animal.'

'I once heard there was a dog let loose in the grounds at Kingsmead Hall every night. That would be the one, then?'

'Yes. After they found Sir Richard's body, Lady Falcon phoned for the police and then told her daugh-ter to get the dog and chain it up. Well, they were all in a state. The daughter was upset, sort of overwrought. She simply forgot about the dog. When the police car arrived there it was by the gate. I understand that it doesn't bark much. It keeps quiet, lying in wait, and it attacks without warning. What you might call a nice quiet animal.'

'So Naylor walked into it?'

'Yes. You know how he is. He couldn't wait. He nipped out of the car instead of telling one of the others, and he was opening the gate when the dog went for him. So *you'll* have to handle the murder, with my help. You'll have both A Div and D Div, and as many men as we can spare for you.'

'Cause of death?'

'A stab wound in the chest. No weapon found. But there's a weapon missing from the Hall. An old sword which was part of a trophy of arms on the wall. It looks as if that might be the murder weapon, but we might know for sure after the doctors have done with the body.'

'Sir Richard Falcon! There'll be an army of reporters.'

'I can take *them* off your neck. Refer all newspapermen to me. I'll have a daily press conference.'

'Right. I'd better go out to Kingsmead.'

'Yes. But first contact Sergeant Errol of D Div. He's waiting for you at Westholme. He handled the preliminaries of the job when Naylor went to hospital.'

'Very good, sir.' Martineau was on his feet. 'Is there anything else?'

'You'll have to remember that the Falcons are very big people, with powerful connections. Don't tread on anybody's corns unless you can't help it.'

Martineau was thoughtful. 'I say,' he said. 'That take-over. Sir Richard was blocking Northern Steel. There are millions at stake. You don't suppose somebody at Northern Steel . . . ?'

'I very much doubt it. I think we'll find it was a thief. Maybe the Dog Man. But of course I could be wrong. You'll have to consider every aspect of the job.'

'The Press will consider that one, all right. Boy, they'll go to town on it. Did Lord Geever stick a sword into Sir Richard Falcon? Ho ho.'

'It's too early for guesses,' said Clay. 'You'd better be on your way.'

Westholme Police Station was D Division Head-quarters. Martineau drove there with Detective Sergeant Devery, and found Detective Sergeant Errol waiting for him. He had always found Errol to be a capable policeman, and he rather liked him. That made no difference to his treatment of him.

'Now then?' he began briskly. 'Anything definite?'

'One or two things, sir,' Errol replied. 'There was a break-in at Kingsmead Hall last night. A piece of glass cut away from a ground-floor window.'

'Like a Dog Man job?'

'Exactly, sir. It could only have been the Dog Man, or somebody who knew the dog very well. P.C. Baines of this division saw the dog loose in the grounds at about a quarter past one, and about ten minutes later he saw a Rolls in the village. It went up towards the Hall, and he thought it was Sir Richard driving home. He's pretty sure, but he couldn't go on oath about it. But it tallies with Sir Richard's movements. He dined at Witchwood Grange with Lord Geever. After dinner they talked business till around one o'clock. Lord Geever saw him to his car, and he drove off a little after one. That puts him easily at Kingsmead at twenty-five past.'

'So he went home and got stabbed. Who found the body?'

'Lady Falcon. She was awakened by the dog howling. I believe it certainly can howl. Baines heard it a mile and a half away.'

'So Lady Falcon went to investigate.'

'Yes. It was turned two o'clock and Sir Richard wasn't in his room. So she went downstairs.'

'They have separate bedrooms?'

'Yes, but that doesn't mean they were not on good terms. It's a way they have in the upper classes.'

'And the body was where?'

'Just inside the front door. Inside the inner door, I mean. There's a sort of nook there which gives a certain amount of concealment. The killer must have been there. Sir Richard wouldn't see him as he came in, but apparently he put his white evening scarf in the hall cupboard, and I suppose that's how he saw the man. He must have gone to tackle him. He was stabbed in the chest.'

'You got Dr. MacKenzie?'

'Of course, sir. And the house was searched thoroughly. Photographs and fingerprints too. They're comparing prints, looking for a stranger's, but they hadn't found anything at the last information. There wasn't a single dab on the window which had been opened.'

'What was stolen?'

'As far as we know, nothing. Except the old sword, which might be the murder weapon. I suppose the thief hadn't had the time to pick anything up.'

'Why would he take the sword away?'

Errol shrugged. 'Your guess is as good as mine. It'll incriminate him if he's found with it.'

'Did anything come out of interrogation?'

'Only what I've told you, sir.'

There was a clean white bandage on Errol's right

hand. Martineau looked at it. 'The dog got you, too?'

Errol grinned. 'Yes, but I've still got all my fingers. I understand it'll be a few weeks before I start biting people myself.'

'I don't think Dr. MacKenzie will allow that to happen.'

'He'll have you put down,' said Devery, who had once been in the same recruits' class as Errol.

There was a laugh. Martineau asked: 'How is Chief Inspector Naylor?'

'Detained in hospital. Serious shock.'

'I should think so, too. Well, I'd better go to Kingsmead and see what's doing. I shall want you on this job with me, but just now you'd better go home and get to bed.'

'Yes, sir. There's just one thing.' Errol's lean, rather handsome face was more than normally serious. He lowered his voice. 'The daughter, Miss Caroline. Her manner was a bit strange. I thought she was heartbroken, but when I searched the house I'm sure I smelled cannabis in her bedroom.'

'She'd been smoking reefers?'

'I thought so, sir.'

'What did you do?'

'Nothing. What could I do in those circumstances?'

'You couldn't do much, with a murder on your hands. But that explains why she forgot to put the dog on the chain. She might have been taking LSD as well. How old is she?'

'Nineteen, sir. And very good-looking.'

'Is that so? All right, I'll go along there. I'll see you later in the day.'

On the way to Kingsmead, Martineau reflected upon the habit of drug-taking. In England the number of drug addicts was increasing, but it was not yet the screaming menace that it was in some parts of the world. And of all the illegal forms of dope, cannabis—also called hashish, Indian hemp, marijuana, pot, and other names—was perhaps the least harmful. Some doctors had even said that it was not habit-forming. Still, it was illegal, and there was always the danger of escalation from cannabis to the really hard drugs. Well, it was a D Division job, and at that moment Martineau was in charge of D Div. C.I.D.

'Well, we'll have to see how it goes,' he mused.

There was a uniformed policeman at the entrance to the Falcon estate, and a second P.C. at the gate to the grounds. This man opened the gates for Martineau's middle-aged Jaguar, and it rolled up the drive between serried battalions of scarlet tulips. Beyond the tulips the lawn stretched away to a rose garden, and beyond the roses, by the far wall of the grounds, there was a solid bank of flowering rhododendrons.

'Lovely, isn't it?' Devery commented.

'You'll have to do better than a Chief Constable before you can have a place like this,' his senior rejoined.

The house was worthy of its setting. Perfectly proportioned in a style which Martineau took to be Georgian, it was large without being ostentatious. The front door was white, and so was the window trim. At the front were four steps up to a terrace which ran the length of the house, and white-painted tubs held azaleas which were a blaze of colour.

'What sort of stone?' Martineau wanted to know.

'The same old millstone grit,' was the reply. 'Pennine stone. Good for a thousand years, I suppose.'

There was no dog in sight, but the front door of the house was standing open. As the Jaguar stopped by the terrace steps a butler appeared. At least he looked like a butler, and he was the first that either policeman had seen in a decade.

They alighted. The butler met them at the top of the steps.

'Good morning, gentlemen,' he said. 'Are you from the police?'

Martineau introduced himself. 'And this is Detective Sergeant Devery. You're the butler, I presume?'

'Yes, sir. My name is Brandon. Will you come in? I'm afraid none of the family is down yet. A very unsettled night.'

'In that case I'll leave the sergeant to chat with you, while I have a wander round outside. Is the dog tied up?'

'Yes, sir. Round the back.' Brandon's plump face was the picture of sympathy. 'It was very unfortunate that he happened to be loose last night. How is the inspector who was mauled?'

'He's in hospital. I expect he'll be all right, though I haven't seen him yet. I'll come back to this door when I want to come in, shall I?'

'Yes, sir, if you please.'

Martineau left the butler with Devery, and he strolled along the terrace in the sunshine. Very soon he found the ground-floor window by which the thief had entered. A clean semicircle of glass had been taken from a pane, near to the window catch. He looked closely, and detected a small brownish smear on the edge of the semicircle. He felt at the cut edge, and touched tiny serrations. He stood looking at the smear, wondering how a man had cut or scratched his hand if he

33

were wearing gloves. He reached carefully through the hole as if to unfasten the catch, and the back of his wrist came in contact with the sharp glass. So it seemed that the burglar had worn gloves with the cuffs turned down. Well, that was something for a start. Somebody had a scratch on the back of his wrist.

He looked at the smooth stone walk beneath the window. There was nothing; not one drop of blood and apparently no dust. He went on his way to the end of the house, where a drive ran along to the back.

He followed the drive into a spacious backyard. Before he reached the rear corner of the house he saw that the coach houses had been turned into garages, though the adjoining stables had not been altered. Curtained windows above the garages indicated that someone lived up there. Both garages and stables were open, and three cars could be seen.

At the corner he looked along towards where he expected the back door to be, and he saw a dog chained to a kennel which looked big enough to house a pony. The dog was lying with its dark head between its forepaws. It was the picture of canine dejection, but it saw Martineau at once. Its head came up and its ears came erect, and it watched the visitor intently.

'All right, boy,' Martineau muttered. '*I'm* not going to come anywhere near you.'

He crossed towards the stables. As he did so a small, spry-looking man in breeches, leggings, and a short-sleeved shirt appeared at the stable door. He watched Martineau in silence.

'Morning,' said Martineau. 'Are you the groom?'

'I'm groom and chauffeur both,' the man said. 'Are you the police?'

Martineau admitted that he was. 'Did you hear anything of the trouble last night?' he asked.

'Not really. They got me out when it was all over. I took the dog from Miss Caroline and fastened him up. I didn't go into the house.'

Martineau raised his glance to the windows over the garages. 'You live up there?'

'Yes. Me and the wife. No kids. I have a phone connected to the house.'

'Did you or your wife hear anything *before* the trouble started?'

'I didn't. And I'm sure the wife didn't because she's talked about nothing else since it happened. If she'd heard anything she'd have mentioned it to me.'

Martineau nodded. He craned a little to look through the stable door. He liked horses. 'Horses in?' he asked.

The chauffeur cocked his thumb over his shoulder. 'They're behind, in the paddock.'

Martineau turned his head and saw that the dog was still watching. 'Does the dog bother them?'

'No. He's got more sense, and so have they. They used to be uneasy with him at one time, but not now.' He sighed. 'I don't know what's going to happen to him. Poor old Rajah. He's right down in the dumps. Sir Richard was the Number One Man with him.'

Martineau was surprised. 'You actually like the dog?'

'Sure. Why not? Everybody is scared of him, but he wouldn't hurt a soul when I was with him. His job is to guard the house. You can't blame him for doing what he's trained to do.'

Martineau said drily: 'It looks as if he slipped-up last night.'

'You don't know that yet, do you? Sir Richard might have brought somebody home with him, though it isn't likely. Or it might have been somebody the dog knows right well.'

'That's possible,' Martineau agreed. He said: 'One of our men heard a dog howling last night. That was Rajah, I believe.'

'I didn't hear it, but I was told it was him. Happen he'd just realised there was something wrong. He's got more sense than some of the folk in the house. You can't blame the dog because somebody was daft enough to leave him loose when the police had been sent for.' There was a sudden, brief silence, and then the chauffeur said quickly: 'Don't tell anybody I said that.'

Martineau grinned. 'I won't mention it to a soul. It was the daughter, wasn't it? Does she drink?'

But now the chauffeur was on his guard. 'Don't ask *me* what she does,' he said. His tone gave the impression that he had more affection for the dog than for Miss Caroline.

Martineau had already ascertained that the man had no scratches on either wrists or hands. He learned that his name was Fletcher, and remarked: 'There's nobody up yet. Have you time to show me the horses?'

'Sure,' said Fletcher. 'This way.'

They went round to the paddock, and looked at two fine, tall hunters and an old pony.

'There's only Miss Caroline rides 'em, now Mr. Peter is away,' said Fletcher. 'The pony is a pensioner. They tell me she rode him when she was a toddler.'

'You didn't work for the Falcon family in those days?'

'No. I'm no old retainer. I've had this job two years. It's all right, I suppose. But it's never right wonderful being in private service. You've got to be respectful no matter what happens. No back answers allowed.'

They were strolling back to the stables.

'You have to take it in the police, too,' Martineau remarked. 'Yes, sir, no, sir. But we don't have to take it from a slip of a girl.'

'Or from her friends,' Fletcher rejoined with a touch of venom. 'Dolled-up corner boys, that's what they are.'

The chief inspector concealed an increasing interest. 'A bit rough, are they?' he asked.

Perhaps he was a little too casual. Fletcher again seemed to remember that he was talking to a detective. 'Well,' he said. 'You might be seeing one or two of 'em. You'll be able to see for yourself.'

They passed along the front of the garages. Martineau looked at the cars, two Rolls-Royces and a little two-seater Triumph which, the chauffeur said, was Miss Caroline's. 'She hasn't killed anybody with it, yet,' he remarked drily.

Martineau would have liked to spend more time with the man, but it occurred to him that he might be absorbing prejudice before he had met any member of the Falcon family. He thanked Fletcher for letting him see the horses, and went on his way round the house. He stayed far enough away from Rajah. The dog showed no sign of hostility, but his unblinking attention was not reassuring. Like most men, Martineau flattered himself that he could get on with dogs. He had no such illusions about Rajah.

5

Coming round to the front of the house again, Martineau stood on the sunny terrace and wished he was there on a more pleasant errand. He thought of Miss Caroline and her 'corner boy' friends whom the chauffeur did not like. Wildish friends and drugs, that was an angle of the case which might be worth considering. It might not be the burglar who had killed Sir Richard Falcon. Indeed, the burglar might have witnessed the killing.

He was standing in thought when Devery and Brandon appeared at the front door.

'This is a pleasant spot on a nice day, sir,' said the butler agreeably.

'It is indeed,' the D.C.I. concurred. 'Is anybody up yet?'

'Her ladyship will be down in five minutes. Would you like to come in?'

They entered the house. Beyond the inner door was a spacious lobby and wide stairs, and through a wide opening on the right was the main hall or living room of the house. On the wall near the foot of the stairs Martineau immediately noticed that a trophy of arms was incomplete.

'Is that where the sword was taken from?' he asked.

'Yes, sir.' The butler's voice was hushed. 'As you'll be able to see, a tallish person could have stood a little way up the stairs and reached the hilt. It would come out of the scabbard easily enough.'

'Somebody in a panic, or a rage,' said the detective. He stepped up a few stairs and reached to where the sword hilt had been. Then he noticed the spot where he had been standing just inside the inner door. There was a chalked outline on the dark carpet.

'It was there, then?' he asked.

'The body? Yes, sir.'

There was no need for the butler to say more. The little recess beside the inner door was where the murderer must have been standing when he was seen.

'Sir Richard would lock the outer door when he came in, I suppose?'

'At that time of night he would, normally. There is no lock on the inner door.'

'So he shut the dog out in the grounds, and he could have been stabbed a few seconds later.' Obviously the murdered man had not been sufficiently alarmed to make an outcry. It had been a quick, quiet, simple, pitiless felony.

'Was the door still locked when the crime was discovered?'

'No. It was unlocked and Sir Richard's keys were in the lock. The murderer could have left the house that way.'

'So we can't be sure that Sir Richard locked the door.'

'No, sir. If he did lock the door, he would probably still have his keys in his hand when he was attacked.'

'Of course. Ah, here comes someone.'

Down the stairs came a woman in her early forties, whom the policemen presumed to be Lady Falcon. That surname was not entirely suitable for her. She was more pretty than handsome, and no doubt more charming than dignified. Of medium height, she had an excellent figure. Her firm neck showed no sign of approaching middle age, and neither did her medium-blonde hair. A dress of satisfactory shortness—by no means a mini skirt—revealed beautiful legs. Martineau thought he discerned a certain tiredness around the eyes, but that was to be expected in the circumstances. Being in the early forties himself, his thought was that she was a damned attractive woman.

The butler made the introductions, and then returned to the front door. Lady Falcon led the way into the big living room. She sat down near a window and invited her guests to be seated also.

'It's my unfortunate duty to ask you some questions, Lady Falcon,' Martineau said.

She nodded rather absently. 'Yes, of course.'

'Did you expect Sir Richard to be late last night?'

'Yes. He said he would probably have a long talk with Lord Geever. They're—they were old friends, you know, but they were in disagreement over a business matter.'

'The proposed take-over?'

'Yes. There's no harm in telling you now. Lord Geever not only wanted Falcon Tools, he also wanted Richard, who was a live wire as you may have heard. But Richard didn't want to be Geever's right-hand man. Though he got on well with Geever, he wanted to be his own man, as he always had been. Last night he expected that Geever would try to talk him round. He said it would be a long session.'

Martineau was surprised. That had been a very full answer from a tired, bereaved woman. Apparently she intended to be as helpful as possible.

'Did you hear him come home?'

'No. He never did make a great deal of noise, and his car is very quiet.'

'The first thing you heard was the dog?'

'Yes. How is poor Inspector Naylor?'

'He's resting in hospital. He'll recover. Now, to return to your husband. Have you thought of any explanation? Any reason for the—crime?'

'Only the obvious one. A burglar caught in the act.'

'That may seem obvious, but it isn't entirely. In a house like this a burglar would be more likely to hide somewhere and let Sir Richard go on up to bed. Can you think of *any* other reason for the crime?'

Lady Falcon shook her head. 'I don't think he had any enemies, of any kind. There was no reason for anyone to do him harm.'

Martineau reflected briefly that the blocked takeover could have been no reason for killing Sir Richard if it were true that Lord Geever's desire to have Sir Richard on his staff had been the main reason for it. He made no mention of this, but pursued: 'There was no sort of trouble in the family?'

Again the lady shook her head. 'None at all. Our son Peter is with his uncle, at Falcon Motors over in Yoreborough. He's getting a thorough training in engineering. He seems quite happy and we have good reports. Our daughter Caroline seems content to stay here with us. Of course she's only nineteen. Richard didn't approve of some of her friends, but the most he did about it was to tell her so. She didn't bring them here when her father was at home, so there was no trouble. He never tried to stop Caroline from going out.'

'Would you think me impertinent if I asked what were *your* feelings about your daughter's friends?'

'No. I think I'm more tolerant than Richard. Some of the young people today are so—so weird, aren't they? Long hair, funny clothes and all that. Richard

41

couldn't stand what he called Beatle types. *I'm* inclined to think that *we* must have seemed just as weird to our own parents.'

'Perhaps we did. These are what we call background questions. Did you and Sir Richard get along all right?'

'Yes. He was a forceful man, but I seemed to be able to manage him. We didn't quarrel.'

'What age was he?'

'Fifty-six.'

'You'll be about sixteen years younger, then?'

'Fourteen. I'm forty-two.'

'You don't look it,' said Martineau. He said it as a fact, and not as a compliment. Also, it occurred to him that the lady was looking out of the window a good deal of the time.

'Are you expecting someone?' he asked.

'Peter. Naturally we sent for him.'

Then she was looking at someone behind him. 'Here comes Caroline,' she said, and he rose to his feet.

Caroline Falcon was obviously 'with it', and very much so. But though she was wearing a dress which looked a little strange to Martineau, he also thought she looked smart. Her fair hair was long and straight like that of thousands of other girls, but with the difference that it was so sleek and glossy that it actually looked heavy. There were no stray rats' tails and no danger of interference with clear vision. The face was attractive, and might some day be beautiful. She was taller than her mother, and not of the same physical type at all.

The two policemen were introduced to her. Her smile seemed to be reluctant, or reserved, and she did not offer to shake hands. Perhaps, Martineau thought, she was shy; or perhaps she could have been shy of police officers.

Then Lady Falcon said: 'Here's Peter,' and she ran to the door. Caroline followed her. Left alone, the two detectives turned to the window. They saw Peter Falcon climbing out of a vintage Bentley, a ferocious, high-prowed old two-seater in shining condition; one of the sort which young men dream about. No doubt it was its owner's pride.

His mother ran to him. He embraced her tenderly, looking properly serious. His sister also ran to him, and he had an arm to enclose her, too. Martineau reflected that he looked like a fine boy. He had a strong likeness to his father, and like his father he was tall and muscular; a thoroughbred Falcon. He would be a Rugger type, without doubt; boisterous at times, but of good behaviour when the occasion called for decorum.

The trio stayed out of doors for several minutes, while Peter heard the story from his mother. Then, still talking, they came in. The mother dried her eyes and asked her son if he had had any breakfast. He replied: 'Not even a cup of coffee. I came right away.' At once Caroline went away to order breakfast. Martineau thought it rather odd that she should do that, in a house presumably full of servants. He wondered: Temporary evasive action?

Not wishing to seem intrusive, Martineau studied the room in which he stood, the hall of Kingsmead Hall. The room was dominated by a portrait above the huge fireplace, and the visitor reflected that it was Sir Richard's father or grandfather still watching the family goings-on. There were bookshelves, though this would not also be the library. The log fire burned cheerfully even on this mild day. There was antique furniture about, and there was plenty of room for it. A huge stand of flowers blazed on the hall table, and papers and magazines were strewn there. The armchairs and settee were big and comfortable, and undoubtedly had been costly when new. It would be a nice room to live in, the detective thought.

Lady Falcon was speaking to him, bringing her son to him.

'This is my son, Peter,' she said with pride. 'These gentlemen are Inspector Martineau and Sergeant Devery.'

There were handshakes. 'I've heard of you, sir,' the young man said to Martineau. 'How do you do?'

'Glad to know you,' said Martineau, impressed by the 'sir'. He recognised it for what it was, the respect shown by a well-bred youngster to a person who was twenty years his senior. A small thing, perhaps, but significant. But Martineau also realised that he might not have noticed it if he had been accustomed to meeting young men of this sort.

'A very sad do,' Peter was saying.

Martineau agreed. 'It's not very nice for you to have policemen hanging around and asking questions at such a time,' he said. 'But the job must be done.'

'You will have all the help we can give you,' said Peter firmly.

Caroline returned, and heard the remark. For some reason she coloured. But she spoke up: 'Breakfast in five minutes.'

Peter thanked her. Martineau said: 'I shall have to talk to some of the staff myself, after I've had a word with Miss Caroline.'

Caroline flushed again. The D.C.I. said: 'There's

no reason to be nervous, miss. Your mother will be with you, if you prefer it that way.'

'You'll be all right with Mr. Martineau, Carol,' her brother said. Then he relaxed and grinned at her. 'Unless he has to ask you about all those comics and flower boys you're running around with. Disgraceful, I call it.'

'They're *not* flower boys,' Caroline flared. 'It's your lot who are disgraceful, with their horrid Rugger songs.'

'Now, children,' said Lady Falcon, though she was smiling. 'Go and get your breakfast, Peter.'

He went off the way Caroline had gone. The policemen were asked to sit, and Martineau began the interrogation of Caroline.

'What time did you go to bed last night?' he asked.

'It would be midnight when I came in. I went straight upstairs.'

'Was everyone else in bed?'

'I suppose so. All was in darkness.'

'You saw the dog when you came home?'

'Yes. He wanted to come into the house, but I shut him out.'

'You went upstairs and straight to bed?'

There was a slight hesitation. 'Yes, more or less.'

'And when were you awakened?'

'The dog woke me, howling.'

'Did you get up?'

'No. I knew that Fletcher or somebody would attend to the dog. I stayed in bed until Mother came to me. She was crying, so I got up at once.'

Tears came to Lady Falcon's eyes, and the girl's eyes brimmed too. The two policemen busied themselves making notes.

In a little while the questioning was resumed. 'Don't think I'm being unnecessarily nosy, Miss Falcon, but where were you until midnight?'

'I was at the Paraguay Club. I left after the floor show.'

Martineau nodded. The Paraguay was one of Granchester's smartest clubs, and it was considered to be respectable. Some people maintained that it was not really a night club, because the last floor show began at eleven o'clock and ended before twelve. After midnight there was gambling, quite legal and well-conducted. Young people who could not afford to play roulette or 'chemmy' were out of the club by midnight.

'Were you alone?' he asked.

'Well, sort of. While the show was on.'

'I see. Before the show one of the artists was with you?'

'That's right. Leo Deluce.'

'Is that a real name, or assumed?'

'It's a stage name, but it's the only one he uses. He thinks his real name wouldn't be suitable.'

'Ah. What is it?'

'Pogson. Leonard Pogson.'

'H'm. What's his line?'

'He sings and plays guitar. With the Seven Foot Four.'

'That's a group, I suppose. It's a peculiar name. Are they all very tall?'

Caroline smiled. 'No, not particularly. There are four of them, but Larry Swann lost a foot in an accident. He wears an artificial foot. So there were four of them with seven real feet between them, and Leo thought of the Seven Foot Four.'

'Are they good performers?'

46

'I think so. They make records. I'm sure they'll soon be in the Top Twenty.'

'And you find that glamorous, I suppose?'

'Well, yes. But they're very nice boys.'

'After the show, did Mr. Deluce bring you home?'

'No.' The girl was suddenly defensive. 'I left him at the club.'

'And you drove home in your own car?'

'Yes. I'm not afraid to be out in the dark.'

'Did you notice anything unusual on your way home?'

'No. Everything seemed to be as usual.'

'Thank you, Miss Falcon. I don't suppose I shall need to bother you again.'

'What about the dog biting the policeman? Will I get into trouble about that?'

'Now I don't know. The circumstances were so unusual, and, one might say, extenuating. I think it might be a good idea if your mother or your brother offered to pay whatever damages there are. That is strictly unofficial advice, and I don't want to be quoted. But it would show a helpful attitude, and it might help.'

'Thank you.'

'Don't mention it. Now I think we'll talk to the staff, if you'll show us where the kitchen is.'

Devery drew him aside. 'I think I might go and look for that sword,' he suggested.

'By all means do,' he was told, and he excused himself and departed.

Lady Falcon led the way to the kitchen. Caroline came along too, and Martineau wondered why. He remembered that he had not asked Lady Falcon about her movements on the previous day, so he took that opportunity.

'I was at home all day,' she said. 'And all evening as well. I went to bed at about half past eleven.'

'Did you hear Miss Caroline come home?'

'No. Sometimes I do, but last night I must have been asleep.'

In the kitchen it was found that the butler, the cook, and two housemaids were the only members of the staff who slept in the house. Martineau questioned them without learning much, though they seemed quite willing to talk. No member of the household knew anything important, apparently. Martineau was not left with any suspicion that it was an inside job, though he did wonder why Miss Caroline had thought it necessary to be present during the interrogation. The girl had *something* on her mind, he felt sure.

Outside there were three gardeners, two men and a boy, and they all lived in the village of Kingsmead. The chief inspector found Munro, the head gardener, showing the boy the proper way to detach an obstinate rose sucker from the stock. He talked to them. Munro was very properly grieved about Sir Richard's death, but he had been sound asleep in bed at the time, and he could give no help. The boy, a well-grown sixteen-year-old, seemed to be in an agony of shyness, and he said not a word.

'He's frightened of strangers,' Munro explained. 'He's that bashful.'

That was when Martineau saw Rajah lurking in the shade of a big shrub. 'Look,' he said in some agitation. 'The dog's loose.'

Munro grinned, and even the bashful boy smiled painfully. Said Munro: 'I've got my eye on him, in case any strangers come. *You* are quite safe, sir. He watched you come out of the house with Lady Falcon.

He never bothers anybody who is a guest of the house.'

But Rajah did not look at all friendly, and Martineau was doubtful. 'Are you sure?' he queried.

'Positive. Happen he was trained that way. He's very intelligent, you know.'

'Do you mean I can now come and go as I like?'

'Not exactly. If you go away and come back this afternoon he *might* challenge you. But after he's been called off and seen you accepted at the house again, he'll accept you too. But don't ever stroke him or touch him. Don't ever lay a finger on him.'

'You need have no fear of that,' said Martineau. 'I wouldn't touch him at any price. How about children, when you have children staying here?'

Munro was shocked. 'My goodness, sir. Rajah wouldn't hurt a child!'

Martineau met the dog's steady, unfriendly gaze, and was sceptical. He said: 'Just you keep your eye on him while I get to my car.'

6

When Martineau reached the entrance to the Falcon estate he saw Devery leaning against the stonework there, apparently waiting for him. The sergeant had a nonchalant air; he seemed to have no pressing problems. Martineau felt sarcastic when he saw him.

'Are you getting your time in all right?' he asked as he stopped the car.

'Quite usefully, sir. I've got something to show you. Here in the grass.'

The D.C.I. stepped out of the car. Devery moved,

and pointed down at something which had been behind him. The grass was longer there, beside the stone of the archway, but the older man had no difficulty in seeing what lay there.

'Have you moved it?' he asked.

'Never touched it.'

'Then somebody didn't try very hard to hide it.'

'No. I thought it would be easy to find.'

'Why?'

'Because it would be left where it would be found.'

'For what reason?'

'So that somebody could put it back where it belonged.'

'You mean the murder was an inside job?'

'Not necessarily. I doubt if this sword was the murder weapon.'

'Then why was it taken?'

'For protection, maybe.'

'Against what?'

'Against a dog, of course.'

'You're way out ahead, aren't you?'

'I'm guessing ahead. Anyway, we've got the sword.'

Martineau used his handkerchief to pick up the weapon. He examined it with interest. The hilt was of steel and leather, and the guard was of steel. The straight blade was bright steel, with no inlay work or engraving. It had been a soldier's sword, not for ceremony but for use.

'How old do you think it is?' he asked.

'Seventeenth century or even older.'

'What gives you that impression?'

'The width of the blade and the thickness of the steel in the guard.'

'Elizabethan, eh?'

'About that time, is my guess. The Spaniards were the top sword-makers then. Toledo steel. So finely tempered that with a rapier the point could be made to touch the hilt, or so they say.'

'This sword might have been worn by one of the Armada men.'

'Originally perhaps. But the Englishman who acquired it would put it to use. Good swords were worth a lot of money. In families of moderate means swords were heirlooms.'

'How do you know all this?'

'I read a book. It was illustrated. Pictures of old swords and muskets.'

'That was the time you were interested in antiques, I suppose?'

'Yes. Do we keep this?'

'For the time being, though there doesn't seem to be any blood on it. We'll give it to Sergeant Bird to test for fingerprints, and then we'll go and have a look at the late Sir Richard Falcon.'

They found Sir Richard's body where they expected to find it, on a slab in the mortuary. Apparently the autopsy had been completed, because Dr. Mackenzie and Dr. Laycock the pathologist were just putting on their coats.

'All done and dusted?' Martineau asked.

Laycock nodded. 'Murder without a doubt. A deep knife wound just below the breast bone. An upward thrust straight into the heart.'

'A knife? Could it have been a sword?'

'A knife with a blade one inch wide at the hilt, and six inches long. It was driven home, very hard. There is an external bruise at the point of entry. There's the body, see for yourself.'

The body was lying on its back. Martineau drew back the mortuary shroud and looked at the wound. Undoubtedly the murder weapon could not have been the sword which was now in Sergeant Bird's possession.

'Until he was stabbed he seems to have been in excellent health,' Laycock continued. 'I couldn't find a thing wrong with him.'

'Thank you,' said Martineau, and the doctors went away.

The dead man's clothes had been sent to the forensic laboratory for routine examination, but the contents of his pockets were still in the custody of the mortuary attendant. Martineau examined them. They seemed to be complete: watch, small cigar case, cigarettes, lighter, a gold pencil, a penknife with a cigar cutter attached, two handkerchiefs, a thin notecase well filled, a cheque book, loose change, a few visiting cards, and a thin pocket diary.

'His keys are in the front door at home,' the D.C.I. said. 'I can't think of anything which might be missing.'

'Credit cards?' Devery suggested.

Martineau looked in the notecase. There were credit cards from the Diners' Club and the Northern Counties Bank.

'Nothing missing, apparently,' he said to the attendant. 'We'll count this money in your presence and give you a receipt for everything. Probably the widow will be able to tell us if anything *is* missing.'

When the two policemen returned to Headquarters, Sergeant Bird reported that the sword had not been wiped clean of fingerprints, but that none of the prints he had found had been good enough for identification purposes.

'The hilt is no good at all,' he said. 'And probably the

fellow who had it had no need to touch the blade. I didn't find any blood. Did you say it was the murder weapon?'

'I did not,' said Martineau. 'And I don't think it was.'

'Well, I've done with it. It can go back where it belongs.'

'All right, bring it here,' was the curt retort.

Martineau spoke on the internal line to Chief Superintendent Clay. The C.I.D. chief wanted to see the sword, probably out of curiosity. Martineau took it along to him, and watched impassively while his stout senior pretended to cut and thrust with it. Then Clay listened to his report without comment, and then proceeded to tell him about the routine work in progress. The sandy road in Kingsmead Wood was being searched for tyre tracks or any other sort of track. Men were nosing about along the fence where P.C. Baines had hunted in the dark. Inquiries were being made in the village itself, and when they were completed the Kingsmead Hall grounds would be thoroughly searched.

'So there you are,' he concluded. 'We want a man with a scratched wrist, and we want to know who was larking about in Kingsmead Wood, and we want to know who borrowed this sword. And there is a possibility that Miss Caroline Falcon has got something on her mind. Are you going to turn up this Seven Foot Four lot?'

'Of course, sir. And I shall have to see what Lord Geever can tell me. Apparently he was the last person to see Sir Richard alive.'

'Apart from the murderer. And that was the Dog Man, for my money.'

'It looks like it, doesn't it?'

'Yes. Now go and see this pop group. *I'm* expecting a visitation of reporters. This lot will be fine for them. A wealthy baronet, a blocked take-over, a howling dog and a seventeenth-century sword. I'll have half Fleet Street here before tea-time.'

'Well, they won't be able to bother Lady Falcon if she stays at home. Not after they hear about the dog.'

'Ah. You've seen it?'

'Yes. And I believe it could kill a man without too much trouble.'

'But not with a knife, eh? Now go and see if you can find a suspect, though my money is still on the Dog Man.'

It was three o'clock in the afternoon when Martineau found Leo Deluce at his flat. Deluce himself answered the door, and the detective realised at once that he was not beholding a typical pop group member. This young fellow was tall and strongly made. His dark, handsome face showed strength. His dark eyes were cool and steady. Still, his black hair was much longer than normal, his white shirt had a frilled front, and his narrow black trousers had a vertical piping of gold brocade. He may not have been a typical pop artist, but at least he was wearing the uniform.

Martineau introduced himself, and asked: 'Are you Leo Deluce?'

With a nod Deluce admitted his identity.

'I'd like to have a little talk with you.'

'All right, Inspector. Come in.'

Martineau passed through a small lobby into a spacious, well-furnished living room. For a bachelor establishment it was surprisingly tidy, and he remarked: 'Very neat.'

'Yes. We have a woman who comes every morning to put the place in order.'

'We?'

'I share this flat with Johnny Revill. He plays guitar with me.'

'In your group?'

'Yes. He's very good.'

Martineau noticed an upright piano and a set of drums. There were several guitars about the place, and they were the only things which marred its orderliness.

'Do you practice here?' he asked.

'Not much, nowadays. We use the club, mainly. But sometimes we gather here to develop a number, when somebody dreams one up. We share royalties and everything.'

'That must be interesting, writing your own songs.'

'Sometimes it is, when it looks like being a good one. We *have* had a couple of good ones.'

Martineau nodded, reflecting that at any rate Deluce did not seem to be hostile. He said: 'I suppose you can guess why I'm here.'

'Because of my friendship with Caroline Falcon?'

'Correct. Naturally we're interested in everything to do with the Falcon family. Did you know Sir Richard?'

'I met him once, just for a few minutes.'

'How did it go?'

'He was civil. But I don't think I was his type.'

'I can understand that. Fathers of daughters can be difficult about young men.'

'Well, I'm not in his class, am I? I was once an

apprentice at Falcon Tools. I don't think he knew that.'

'You've got a trade in your fingers, then?'

'Two, if you count the guitar.'

'No. The guitar is a profession. There's a Spaniard playing at the Tahiti Club. I hear he's very good.'

'Spain is the place where they *really* play the guitar. They still make the best ones, too. I think I ought to go and hear that Spaniard.'

'Were you with Caroline last night?'

The question was abrupt, but Deluce did not blink. 'Yes,' he said. 'She was at the club.'

'Until what time?'

'Going up to midnight.'

'Did you see her home?'

'No. I was tired.'

Martineau considered Deluce. He looked quite fit. The query came: 'Too tired to take your girl home?'

'She has a car. I have a car. There was no sense in two cars going out to Kingsmead. I could have ridden out in her car, and walked back. I don't much care for walking.'

Martineau appeared to accept that. But the excuse of tiredness by a young fellow who was used to late hours had been the first utterance of the interview which had seemed to him not quite true. Of course his story tallied with Caroline's. There had been time for her to arrange that.

'So she went home alone. What did you do?'

'I went home too. And to bed.'

'Did your team-mates come home too?'

'No. I don't know what they did. They were at the club when I left.'

'What do you call them?'

'Johnny Revill, like I said. Larry Swann plays piano. Pete Wallace is drums.'

'Where do those two live?'

'They have a flat in the house next door.'

'Did you hear any of them come home?'

'No,' said Deluce, with a hint of weariness.

That was a normal reaction to a lot of questions. Martineau shifted his ground. 'How do you get on with the dog at Kingsmead Hall?'

'We're not on speaking terms, but he's never tried to bite me.'

'Have you been out there quite often?'

'Three times. Once when I met Sir Richard. After that Caroline didn't take me home when he was around. I was there twice more in the afternoon. Lady Falcon was there.'

Martineau nodded. He said: 'I have to be nosy, you know. How serious is this affair between you and Caroline?'

'*I'm* serious enough. I'd marry her tomorrow if I could.'

'When this new law for eighteen-year-olds comes in, she won't need parental permission.'

'No. But it isn't in yet. Anyway, I can't ask her yet, with the old man murdered.'

'So you're prepared to wait a while?'

'Yes. I can wait.'

'How old are you?'

'Twenty-three.'

'You're plenty young enough,' said Martineau, and he made his departure. He went out of the flat reflecting that something about Leo Deluce was not quite right. And he certainly had had a motive for murder. It was not out of the question to presume that Sir

Richard Falcon would have firmly and furiously forbidden his daughter to marry a man like Deluce. With the coming of the new law, she could have married against his wishes. In that case, Sir Richard would have made sure that his daughter would have enough money to support herself, with none to spare for Deluce. She would have had no great fortune.

But now Sir Richard was dead. The great obstacle to a wealthy marriage for Deluce had been removed. Now, he could afford to wait until after the will had been read.

Martineau mused that Leo Deluce might not be the main suspect in the Falcon case, but he was certainly not in the clear.

7

At the street door Martineau met another long-haired young man who was about to enter. He stood in the way. 'Does your name happen to be John Revill?' he asked.

'Yes, I'm Johnny Revill,' the man replied.

'You live here with Leo Deluce?'

'Live with him? We share a flat.'

Martineau smiled. 'I wasn't inferring that you were a couple of queers. I'm Chief Inspector Martineau of the city police.'

'Yes. I know who you are.'

'I'm making inquiries about Mr. Deluce, because of his friendship with a member of the Falcon family.'

'Well, what is it you want to know? Leo's life is an open book.'

'Ah. You're a great friend of his?'

'Yes. I think I can say that.'

'Well, you're forthright at any rate,' said Martineau to himself. He studied the man, whose direct gaze met his fearlessly. Like Deluce, he was tall and well built. His dark hair, like Deluce's, was worn long. He was handsome like Deluce, and he had a small moustache like Deluce. The two men could have been brothers. But this one wore a white tunic with gold braid on cuffs and epaulettes. It definitely had a military appearance.

'What army was that?' he asked.

Revill grinned. 'I got it in Carnaby Street,' he said. 'I think it had belonged to some comic opera army. But I had the trousers made.'

Martineau looked down at red drainpipe trousers with gold piping. 'Very nice,' he said politely. 'Were you an engineering apprentice, too?'

'No. I was trying to sell furniture.'

'How old are you?'

'Twenty-three.'

'Does Mr. Deluce take after you, or do you take after him?'

'I dunno. We have similar tastes, except in girls. I don't go for blondes.'

'Then you won't quarrel over women. I presume you were at the Paraguay Club last night?'

'Yes. I'm there every night, bar Sunday.'

'Was Caroline Falcon there with Deluce?'

'Well, he sat at her table between shows.'

'Was she there when you finished your act?'

'Yes. I believe she was.'

'Can you remember what time she went?'

'To tell you the truth, I can't remember. Three of

us, Larry Swann, Pete Wallace and I went to the Tahiti Club to see this Spanish act they've got. Very good.'

'How long did you stay there?'

'Late-ish. Between two and three.'

'What time did Deluce get home?'

'*I* don't know. I expect he was in bed when I got home. I didn't go into his room to find out.'

'You saw him this morning at breakfast time?'

'No. We're night birds, you know. We don't eat breakfast. Lunch is the first meal of the day.'

'Did you have lunch together?'

'Today we did. I got an early edition of an evening paper, and the murder was mentioned.'

'Did Deluce tell you what time he went to bed?'

'No. I never asked him. What time does he *say* he went to bed?'

'Before midnight.'

For a brief moment Revill showed surprise. Then he shrugged. 'If that's what he says, I suppose it's right.'

'Does he often go to bed early?'

'No,' Revill had to admit. 'It's no use saying he does. You could find out if you wanted.'

Martineau nodded. 'When you saw the news of the murder in the paper, you talked about it with Deluce?'

'Naturally. Caroline's father.'

'Didn't you ask about her?'

'I did, but not right away. As soon as Leo saw the paper he dashed off to phone Caroline. When he came back I asked him if she was all right. He said she was. He said she was asleep in bed when it happened.'

'Where did this conversation take place?'

'In the bar at the Stag's Head. We were just having the odd one before lunch.'

'Then Deluce phoned from there?'

'Yes, I expect so. No reason for him to go anywhere else to phone.'

'Thank you, Mr. Revill. How has Deluce been since that time?'

'Just the same. *He* wasn't broken-hearted about Old Man Falcon. Though I expect Caroline is.'

Martineau thanked the young man again, and let him go. He drove away from there, still reflecting that Leo Deluce's early-to-bed story did not ring true.

At Headquarters he instructed Sergeant Devery to seek out Larry Swann and Pete Wallace, to find out if they would tell the same story as Johnny Revill. Devery went on the errand at once, and returned with corroboration of Revill's statements. Deluce could not be reached through his friends, but neither could they give him any sort of alibi.

Martineau went to see Lord Geever. He was ushered into the great man's office at Northern Steel. It was a splendid office, and Lord Geever was an awe-inspiring man. But he and Martineau had met before, and he greeted the policeman as if he were glad to see him. . . .

'You've come about Falcon, I suppose,' he said. 'Poor old Dick. I've known him most of my life.'

Martineau agreed that it was a sad thing, and then he had to answer, or appear to answer, a number of questions about aspects of the murder which had not been made public. Lord Geever was like anyone else. He liked to have inside information.

'Of course you know he left my house and went straight to his death,' the peer said when he thought he had learned all that the police knew. 'We had a long session here after dinner. I talked to him like a Dutch uncle, but to no avail.'

'I hope you parted friends,' Martineau said.

'Oh yes. Mind you, I was cross with him. He was a stubborn old rascal. But I hadn't given up hope.'

'Did he know you were cross?'

'Of course. He only laughed at me. We were *very* old friends, you know. We've fallen out many a time, but now we've got to the age where we can't insult each other. Or I should say, we *had* got to that age. It was a great blow to me, I can tell you. A great blow.'

Martineau looked at this old man who was years older than Sir Richard Falcon had been. He was big and florid, and he had a reputation for working hard and living hard. But his small blue eyes were bright and clear, and it was said that he still played a good game of snooker without glasses, and that without any aid to vision he was still better than most young men with a twelve-bore. He was supposed to be as cunning as a fox and as hard as nails, but that could be the reputation of any man who has successfully ruled a huge industrial corporation for thirty years. Obviously he had been really hurt by an old friend's death, but no doubt he would now be reflecting on the improved prospects of a take-over of Falcon Machine Tools.

Martineau heard all that he had to say about Sir Richard Falcon, and was preparing to take his leave, when Geever said innocently: 'I expect you've been to see Robbie Weston?'

'Er, no,' the detective replied. 'Who is Robbie Weston?'

'I hope I haven't put my foot in it,' Geever said, but there was mischief in his eye. 'This *is* confidential, isn't it?'

'It is, unless it's evidence.'

'Well, I wouldn't call it evidence. Robbie Weston is the Falcon Company Secretary. He is also a director and a friend of the family.'

'I see. Thank you. I'll go and see what he has to say.'

Geever cleared his throat, and looking at him Martineau realised that there was now no doubt about the mischief. 'I have heard it said,' Geever volunteered, 'that Weston was more friendly with Lady Falcon than he was with Falcon.'

Martineau merely nodded, and thanked the man again. He departed remembering something else about Lord Geever. In his younger days he had been reputed to be something of a devil with the ladies.

Now then, he thought. Was that jealousy, or what?

At Falcon Machine Tools Robert Weston found that he had time to see Chief Inspector Martineau. They shook hands and exchanged the proper remarks about it being a sad affair. Weston appeared to be about fifty years old; a very fit and good-looking fifty. Seeing him, the visitor remembered where he had heard his name. Weston had been a golfer of considerable local renown.

Martineau said, referring to this: 'What is your handicap these days, sir?'

Weston smiled. 'I'm still marked down to two, but I can't often play to it. Do you play?'

'Occasionally. It's something I hope to take up when I retire.'

'Good. It'll keep you fit. Now . . .' Weston looked at his watch. 'I suppose you'll be wanting to know how the firm's affairs could possibly have affected this sad happening.'

'I'm wanting to know anything there is to know.'

'Ah. No suspects yet?'

'There is one obvious suspect, when we can lay hands on him. We generally find in these matters that the obvious person is the culprit, but we're investigating all aspects. Is it likely that the proposed take-over could have had anything to do with it?'

Weston shook his head. 'Naturally I've thought about it. But the fight wasn't as bitter as all that. It wasn't anybody's neck. Besides, the important thing to Northern Steel was to get Sir Richard into their organisation. To kill him didn't make sense.'

'What was your position in the matter?'

'I was strongly against the take-over. And it's no secret that I still am.'

'You supported Sir Richard, then?'

'Yes. Wholeheartedly.'

'You were friends?'

'Yes. Since boyhood.'

'You were the same age?'

'I was two years younger. I'm fifty-four.'

'You don't look it,' said Martineau, and again he was stating a fact. 'You'll know the whole family, then?'

'Yes. I'm godfather to Peter Falcon. *Sir* Peter, he is now. Richard was a baronet.'

'Would you know Lady Falcon before she was married, then?'

'Yes.' Weston took the question as a matter of course.

'Are you married?'

'I was. I've been six years a widower.'

'Grown-up children?'

'No. Childless.'

'So you would naturally be interested in your god-son's career.'

'Of course.'

'You would of course know that Sir Richard was dining with Lord Geever last night?'

'Yes. He came into this office and told me. I told him he would be under some pressure. He said: "I know. But it won't change anything." '

'Did you see him again after that?'

'No. I never saw him again.'

'Did you see any others of the family that day?'

'Yes. I called and had a drink before dinner with Virginia. That's Lady Falcon. I'd told Richard I would, because he'd said she would be alone all evening. That would be about seven o'clock, and I stayed till about a quarter to eight.'

'Then where did you go?'

'Home. My housekeeper Mrs. Hawkins served dinner at eight. You'll find her address in the phone book. She lives in Highfield somewhere.'

'I live in Highfield, and I know a Mrs. Hawkins. A widow woman, about sixty.'

'That will be her. Small, quiet, and well spoken.'

'The same, I'm sure.'

'She makes me dinner Tuesday, Wednesday, and Thursday. Other days I dine out somewhere.'

'I'll check with her, but it's just routine, Mr. Weston.'

'I understand that you always have to check if you can.'

That was the end of the interview. Martineau went away, and he was inclined to think that Lord Geever's insinuation about Weston had been groundless gossip.

But of course he would not forget it.

In this case, he thought, there had not yet been anything for a policeman to get hold of, and shake. 'Dog Man, where art thou?' he begged silently. 'Let us have a look at you.'

8

There was a time when the British policeman stood head and shoulders above the crowd. Nowadays, though many policemen are still big men, the physical superiority is not so noticeable.

That is because the physique of the population at large has improved tremendously in the last two decades. There are not many proud fathers in England today whose grown-up sons are not taller than themselves. A race of people which was inclined to be short and sturdy has become—or is becoming—bigger and heavier.

In contrast to this, the shortage of police recruits has made Chief Constables less choosy than they used to be. They have to take what they can get. While there are a great many large young men about, not many of them are anxious to be policemen. As a result of this, there has been a lowering of minimum physical standards. Nowadays, there is a small percentage of younger officers who are only of medium physique. But in a police force whose members do not carry firearms, there seems to be as much need for physical strength as ever there was. However plucky and well-trained he might be, the smaller member of the force occasionally finds himself facing a problem which he is not big enough to tackle successfully.

During the short nights of May in northern England, the darkest hours are certainly dark enough. And in the residential suburb of Parkhulme in Granchester, where the grounds of big houses have high walls overhung by trees, there are corners distant from street lights which can be very dark indeed.

On a still, dark night, it is sometimes rewarding for a policeman on his beat to stand in shadow and listen for a while. Four nights after the night of the Falcon murder, P.C. Albertson of D Division was doing precisely that at five minutes to one in the morning, in Russop Drive, Parkhulme. He had just decided that it was time for a smoke when he heard a noise.

Russop Drive was an unmade, unadopted road with a sandy surface. There were loose stones here and there, and Albertson guessed that, somewhere in the vicinity, somebody had kicked a small stone and sent it rolling a little way. He stood quite still, waiting. Distantly he heard a rushing car as it passed the end of Russop Drive. There was no other sound.

Eventually Albertson discerned movement between himself and a distant street light. He knew that it was not a superior officer seeking him. His sergeant would have uttered a soft, distinctive whistle; the inspector would have struck the stone kerb with his stick.

He saw movement again, and it was nearer. Someone was coming towards him. He waited, standing close to a high garden wall. He was not expecting trouble. It was probably a late wayfarer who had had a drink or two.

But as the shadowy figure came nearer, Albertson discerned a certain furtiveness. This character was sneaking along close to the wall, in the deepest shadow.

That was not the manner of an honest citizen making his way home.

When he thought that the stranger was about to become aware of his presence, Albertson snapped on his torch. The bright beam picked out a man wearing dark clothes and a beret. The man stopped, staring at the light. He showed no emotion as Albertson approached him.

'Evening,' Albertson said.

The man did not speak.

Albertson made a quick physical assessment. The man was about six feet tall, and well built; not quite a heavyweight but certainly bigger than a middleweight. His arms were long, and his hands looked big and capable. He seemed to be something under thirty years old, and Albertson thought he was potentially a rough customer.

'You're out late,' the P.C. said. 'Do you live around here?'

The man shook his head. His dark face was expressionless.

'Then what are you doing here at this time of night?'

The answer was a shrug. Albertson felt baffled, and he realised that there was indeed going to be trouble. He was the smaller man. His 5 feet 8½ inches without shoes, and his thirty-eight-inch chest, normal, had just been enough to cover the recently reduced physical requirements for the force.

'I think you'd better explain yourself,' he said.

Again the answer was a shrug.

Albertson was no coward. 'In that case you'd better come with me, and we'll see what . . .'

At that moment he was surprised by a very old trick. He was not tensed for action because he had not yet finished speaking. He had expected to make the first move by getting hold of the man, especially since the man had lowered his glance in a crestfallen way.

The stranger had not been crestfallen. He had merely been looking at Albertson's torch, and now he lunged forward and grabbed it. The torch was heavy, rubber-covered, designed for use as both club and flashlight. The P.C. had been holding it ready for use as a club. The stranger seized it by the bulbous end, and before Albertson realised it, it was gone from his hand. A second later he was being beaten with it. A heavy swipe across the lower part of the face shook him. He tried to close with his assailant, but a long left arm held him off. He seized the arm with both hands, and attempted to get into position for a wrestling throw. The club was brought up deftly to the rear brim of his helmet. The helmet fell to the ground with a hollow thump, and that was the loudest noise of the fight. The beam of the torch went up and around like a demented searchlight as the stranger beat the policeman's head with it.

Albertson recovered consciousness half an hour later. He would have immediately reported his predicament to divisional Headquarters if he had been able to find his personal radio. But the stranger had taken it, or had thrown it away.

He tottered to the main road, and collapsed on the short roadside grass. Eventually a police motor patrol stopped and picked him up.

The rubber-covered torch had not been designed to break men's heads. The shaken condition of the brain known as concussion was Albertson's trouble. He lay in hospital and kept his head very still, because it hurt him to move it. But he could listen and answer questions, and his memory seemed to be unimpaired.

Martineau was not contemptuous of this young man who had probably met the Dog Man face to face and allowed him to get away. Albertson was not the first policeman to have accosted a wayfarer in suspicious circumstances, and then to have found that he had caught a Tartar. It was just a pity that this particular Tartar had not been met by a stronger and more experienced officer.

The chief inspector listened to Albertson's story, and perceived how he had been taken by surprise. He got a good description of the stranger, because the P.C.'s memory of the man was vivid. 'The most unforgettable character I ever met,' he joked weakly.

'How was he dressed?' came the question.

'Blue or black beret, blue donkey jacket, and some filthy old overalls. You could see they were scruffy even in the dark. I never noticed his shoes.'

Martineau did not have much faith in Identikit, but he sent an artist to the hospital to co-operate with the injured man in producing a likeness. To his surprise the two men did produce a drawing which looked like somebody, though Albertson said that it wasn't quite right. A copy of the hard, expressionless face was issued to every member of the Granchester force, and then Martineau hoped for the best.

The missing personal radio was found a short distance away from the scene of the crime, but it carried no fingerprints and there were no other clues. Albertson's torch was not found.

There had been no burglaries in Parkhulme or anywhere else in the city on the night of Albertson's misfortune, so it seemed likely that the P.C. had stopped the Dog Man before a crime, and not after it. Because of the semi dead-end quality of Russop Drive, the suspect could not have been going anywhere but to one of the neighbouring houses when he was stopped. One of those houses had been his target. Martineau caused inquiries about dogs to be made in that vicinity. At three out of eight big houses male canines were kept. Since all the Dog Man's jobs had occurred at houses where dogs and not bitches were kept, the three houses in Russop Drive were put down for Special Vigilance, because it was thought that the Dog Man might just be persistent enough to make a second attempt at burglary in Russop Drive.

Detective Chief Inspector Naylor of D Division came out of hospital but remained on the sick list. Martineau paid him a comradely visit at his home.

'I thought I'd let you get home before I bothered you,' he said.

'Oh, you're welcome,' Naylor said. 'How's the job going?'

'Dead slow,' was the honest reply. 'But we're just a shade nearer to the Dog Man. When we get him, I think the Falcon job will clear itself.'

Naylor nodded his agreement with that opinion. He very gently tapped the upholstered arm of his chair with his bandaged right hand.

'What's up?' Martineau asked. 'Are you sweating to get back to work?'

Naylor grinned, and touched the scar on his face. 'I'd frighten every baby and old lady in the division. Besides, this hand is a mess. I don't believe we're down to using one-handed coppers yet. Also, I don't mind you or anybody else carrying the can for the Falcon job. If you don't find the Dog Man, your name's McCoy.'

'Oh, I'll find him.'

Naylor laughed, and quoted a police hand-out phrase: 'At any moment we expect to make an arrest.'

Martineau grinned, and said: 'You could have been worse off. At any rate the dog was clean. I understand there's no infection.'

'Oh, I shall be all right, except they'll call me Scar-face.'

'Will it be bad?'

Naylor shrugged. 'It won't matter if my wife can stand it. I don't chase the girls around any more.'

'The scar might lend you a touch of distinction, like a German duellist. Any hard feelings about the dog?'

'I don't think I'd like to meet him again.'

'Have you considered any sort of action?'

'Not seriously. The dog was doing his job, and he was on his own midden. You can't blame *him*. There was negligence in not fastening him up when the police had been sent for, but look at the circumstances. Every-body in a state about the murder. I don't see how you can blame anybody really. Anyway, I wouldn't want to be the man to bring any more trouble to Lady Falcon at this time.'

'You know her?'

'I know her about as well as somebody like me *could* know her. She's a nice woman.'

'How about the daughter, Caroline?'

'I suppose she's all right. I don't know anything about her.'

'Except what Sergeant Errol told you.'

'The reefer smoking? There's only what Errol

thought he could smell. Have you done anything about it?'

'Not yet. Like you, I don't want to bring any more trouble to Lady Falcon just now. Besides, I've got my hands full with murder and robbery. They make reefers seem a bit trivial.'

'Reefers aren't trivial if they lead people on to cocaine and heroin.'

'There doesn't seem to be any of that with Caroline and her crowd. Not yet, at any rate. Still, I suppose we'll have to do something eventually. We ought to have a Narcotics Squad, even if it were only three or four men. Then they could fool about with the job.'

'Two men and two women, specialising, could do a lot of good,' said Naylor thoughtfully.

Martineau perceived the conversation was slanting itself towards mere police gossip. Appearing to accept that, he said casually: 'Do you know this fellow Robbie Weston?'

'No. Who's he?'

'A director of Falcon Tools, that's all.'

Naylor was not a detective chief inspector for nothing. 'Then why mention him?' he asked shrewdly. 'What's the angle on him?'

'I got a broad hint from a so-called friend of the Falcon family that Weston was also a good friend of the family, and more of a friend of the wife than the husband. I had a talk with Weston, but didn't get anywhere with him. He seemed honest enough.'

'Lady Falcon is a good-looking woman. You always get gossip of some sort. Who was your informant?'

'It was confidential.'

'It wasn't that Seven Foot Four character, was it?'

'Leo Deluce? No.'

'I also have an informant. In Kingsmead Hall. But I never heard a Weston mentioned.'

'Is it the butler?'

Naylor grinned and shook his head. 'Confidential,' he said.

'I'll bet it was one of the distaff side of the staff. What *did* you get to know?'

'Nothing of any real use. You get a lot of prejudice from old retainers. Miss Caroline is not universally beloved. She's a bit thoughtless with the servants. And her friends are not liked. Seemingly she's letting the family down.'

'But no mention of narcotics?'

'No. Drink has been mentioned. With bated breath. Apparently it's a great sin.'

'Well, she's only nineteen.'

'I wish I was nineteen again. I wouldn't be a copper.'

And Martineau perceived that there would be no more information from Naylor, whether or not he had any to give.

9

Ever since the night of the Falcon murder, P.C. Baines had been specially vigilant when his patrol took him to Kingsmead. Not only was he vigilant, he was expectant. He felt sure he was going to see more of the person who had eluded him that night. It was not a logical expectation, because it was unlikely that the Dog Man would come again to Kingsmead Hall. Nor was the night lurker likely to have been a poacher. The small Kingsmead Hall herd of deer was still intact. There were a few hares around there, but scarcely any game birds. Still, Baines was expectant. In his own words, he felt it in his bones.

Every night of that fine May, when he was in Kingsmead the P.C. spent as much time as he could spare watching the entrance to the Hall drive from a place of concealment. Also, before he left the village, he rode out to the boundary and made sure that no car was parked in the little lane in Kingsmead Wood. His simple intention was that if there was anything to see, he was going to see it.

His patience was rewarded by an incident which he called a 'suspicious occurrence'. At a quarter past midnight one warm, dry night he saw Caroline Falcon drive her two-seater past the entrance to the Falcon estate and on towards the city boundary. Her car was followed by a Mini-Cooper which could have been anybody's car. Ignoring that, Baines pondered about Miss Falcon. 'Going to a party somewhere, I expect,' he decided. She had been alone in the open car.

Five minutes later the two-seater returned, and went through the gateway to Kingsmead Hall. There were two people in it. The driver still seemed to be Miss Caroline, and the other person also had shoulder-length hair. It could have been a girl, but Baines was more inclined to think it was that Leo Deluce he had heard about.

When the car had gone he pondered: 'What's the game?' He went to the place where his motor-cycle was hidden, and he rode out to the boundary and into the wood. In the little sandy lane he found a Mini-Cooper with a warm radiator. The car was locked. He inspected the Road Fund licence and made a note of the car's number. Then he spoke to his division by radio.

'I just found a car parked in Kingsmead Wood,' he said. 'Not far from where I saw somebody on the night of the murder.'

The station sergeant was informed. He came to speak to Baines. 'In the wood, you said?' he queried. 'You're over the boundary.'

'About three hundred yards,' said Baines, who knew he had full powers up to five hundred yards beyond the boundary.

'What made you go rooting around there?'

Baines told the sergeant about Caroline Falcon's unusual trip into the wood, and about her return with a passenger.

'She'll be sneaking him into the house for a quiet canoodle,' the sergeant decided. 'Spend some time around there and see what happens.'

But Kingsmead Hall had been mentioned. The sergeant informed D Division C.I.D., which was represented at that time by Sergeant Errol, Detective Constable Cooper, and the detective in reserve.

Errol remembered that someone had been in Kingsmead Wood on the night of the Falcon murder, and not much before the estimated time of the murder. He said to the station sergeant: 'Cooper and I will have a run out to Kingsmead.'

At Kingsmead Errol stopped the car near to the private road. The village was quiet, and nothing stirred. He got out of the car, making himself recognisable to a watcher. At once Baines showed himself, and came to the car.

'Nothing's happened since I rung in,' he reported.

Errol thought about that. 'Well,' he said. 'We don't

want anybody to think they're being kept under observation. We'll have two Traffic cars. One at the other side of the wood and one on this road back to town. They'll stop the mini and say it's a routine check, and see who's driving it.'

'I have the car's number,' said Baines.

'The car could be borrowed. We want to know who's driving it. We'll put our car behind the pub, and go up towards the house. We might see this bod come out of the gate. Does that damned dog make a noise?'

'I've never known it to bark. It just waits to get hold of you and tear you to bits.'

'Right,' said Errol. He got into the car and gave his instructions, then drove his car into the yard of the Falcon Arms. When he returned, Baines asked: 'And what do *I* do?'

Errol was silent for a moment. He had not given Baines a job, and that was unfair. In a manner of speaking, the entire job was Baines's.

'You hide somewhere near the car in the wood,' Errol said at last. 'See if you can figure out which way the fellow comes on foot. He might come across the fields.'

The only cover anywhere near to the closed gates of Kingsmead Hall was a big old beech tree. Cooper was the taller of the two detectives, and the sergeant climbed on his back and shoulders to reach the lowest branch. From there he was able to reach down to Cooper's outstretched hands, and with a good deal of grunting and scuffling the taller man was enabled to join him in the tree. Both men found fairly comfortable perches. They could see the gate in starlight some eighty yards away. They also saw the dog Rajah come to the gate, apparently to stare out through the bars. Neither man moved or spoke, but both of them had the same thought, that the dog had heard them struggling to get into the tree, and had come to investigate.

The detectives remained completely still until Rajah went away from the gate. Or at least he seemed to go away.

'Ah,' breathed Cooper. 'Are we having a smoke?'

'No,' was the whispered reply. 'That dog is dead crafty.'

Denied a chance to smoke, Cooper reflected that since the damned dog had had the audacity to maul a chief inspector, sergeants and such were starting to think that it was ready to put up for the city council. He settled down to wait, as still and as quiet as Errol.

It was a longish vigil. When a distant clock struck the hour of two, Errol whispered: 'We should have been signing off now.'

Cooper replied: 'They're having a long session. She hasn't taken a fellow indoors just for a kiss and a squeeze.'

'They could do that in the car.'

'They can do lots of things in a car.'

'Yes. But if they smoke reefers in a car they're taking a big chance of being caught.'

'I never smelled a reefer.'

'You will, one of these days.'

'Do they smoke the reefers before or after?'

'Before or after what?'

'You know. The love session.'

'Don't ask me. I was never invited to a pot party.'

Thereafter was silence, and at about half past two there was movement on the other side of the gate. Two people were there, and the dog. One of them appeared to be wearing a long coat, and this person seemed to be holding the dog by the collar. The second person was taller, bigger altogether. Errol guessed that it was a girl and a man, and the girl was wearing a dressing gown.

There was no long farewell. The man opened the gate and slipped through, closing it quietly. If anything was said, it could not be heard by the men in the tree. The man moved away from the gate, and away from the driveway. He moved silently on grass, towards a field gate. He lightly vaulted the gate, and went away across the field, moving in the direction of Kingsmead Wood. The girl and the dog stayed watching until he was out of sight, then they too went away.

There was silence in the beech tree, until Errol whispered: 'He never even kissed her Good Night.'

'No,' Cooper replied. 'The dog might not like it.'

Police Constable Baines chose to wait at a spot equidistant from the field gate which led into the wood, and the little car which waited in the lane. He was not a particularly patient man, but he was an experienced policeman and therefore not unused to long vigils. He allowed himself an occasional cigarette, to break the monotony which makes a man sleepy.

He also heard the clock strike two, and like his colleagues in plain clothes he thought that the lovers were having a long session. That is, if they were lovers. He reminded himself that there had been some funny aspects of the Falcon job. Those two might not be lovers at all.

About half an hour later Baines did begin to lose patience. 'Is the bloke staying the night, or what?' he asked himself. He thought about the possibility of that, and then he moved towards the field gate, to see if there was anything stirring in that direction.

He was no more than five yards from the gate when a man appeared there and lightly vaulted over. He could not fail to see Baines standing in front of him on the lane's sandy surface. No doubt he was as surprised as the policeman. He stood quite still while the latter inspected him by flashlight.

'Now then,' said Baines. 'What are you doing here?'

The man did not answer. Baines approached him. He spoke in his most official manner. 'In view of recent happenings around here, I demand an explanation from you.'

The man moved suddenly. He tried to get by, handing off the policeman with a stiff right arm. He did not succeed. His arm was caught by the wrist, in a powerful grip. He turned, and swung his left fist. Baines received a painful but by no means stunning blow under the ear. His flashlight was of the rubber-covered clubtorch type. He used it to hit the arm he held, numbing it. Then with an adroit and rather contemptuous pull-and-push, he turned his opponent, then kicked him behind the knee and threw him to the ground. He straddled the man while he handcuffed him.

'Don't start trying to play your lads' games with me,' he reproved. 'I know you. You're Leo Whatsisname. I ought to give you a thick ear, but the job might be too important. Come on, get up.'

On his feet, Leo Deluce asked dully: 'Am I under arrest?'

'Too true, you are. Assault on police will do for a start. And if you try any more tricks I shall have to thump you in self-defence.'

Deluce sighed. 'I'll go quietly. You can take these things off me.'

Strangely enough Baines believed him. Also he thought that the handcuffs were a little too drastic in the circumstances. He took the precaution of making sure that Deluce was unarmed, and then he released his wrists.

They walked to the car. Baines unlocked it with Deluce's key. With his prisoner sitting beside him he drove to Kingsmead, where he saw Errol and Cooper beside the inn. He stopped.

Errol looked to see who was in the car, and asked: 'Who's that you've got?'

'A chap called Leo Deluce. I asked him a civil question and he tried to run for it. I caught him and he thumped me.'

'Did you thump him?'

'Not where it shows. You know I'm not violent, Sarge.'

'He's under arrest, I presume. Assault?'

'That's it. Unless there should be something else turn up.'

'Well, somebody will want to talk to him. Let me drive him in. You follow on your bike, and Cooper can bring in our car.'

'Right you are, Sarge.'

10

At the Westholme police station of D Division, Leo Deluce was searched, but the business of charging him with Assault on Police was delayed while Sergeant Errol suspiciously pondered the circumstance that there was a gold cigarette lighter among the prisoner's personal property, but no cigarettes.

'What, no gold fag case?' Errol queried.

'I'd smoked up,' Deluce said.

'Ah. We'll just go out and look at your car. Bring your torch, Baines.'

Errol, Baines, Cooper and the prisoner went out into the police station yard, where the Mini-Cooper stood. Behind the front seat, pushed out of sight, Baines found a gold cigarette case.

'Ah,' said Errol with menacing geniality. 'You thought we were a lot of mugs, did you? Now you can't say *we* dumped this, can you? Gold cig cases are a bit out of our reach. *You* dumped it, didn't you? Well now, I'm going to carry it on the flat of my hand into the charge room, so as you can keep your eye on it all the way. Just to prove we're on the level. Let's go.'

Deluce was silent. The four men trooped back into the station, where Errol opened the gold case. It contained nine Senior Service cigarettes and three cigarettes which appeared to be home-made.

'Been rolling your own, I see,' said Errol. 'Now then, you are not obliged to say anything in answer to my questions, but anything you do say will be taken down in writing and may be used in evidence. Now, what's special about these home-rolled ones?'

Deluce shrugged. 'I don't know. They're not mine.'

'The case is yours, I take it?'

'Yes, it's my case.'

'The Mini-Cooper is yours?'

'Yes, it's my car.'

'In your case, in your car. Therefore in your possession, wouldn't you say?'

Deluce was silent.

'What are these cigarettes?' Errol persisted.

Again Deluce shrugged. 'I told you they were not mine.'

'Did you know they were in the case?'

Deluce could be seen to consider. It was he who had hidden the case. Therefore he had had a reason. He said: 'Yes, I knew.'

'Who put them there?'

There was no reply.

'Let's begin at the beginning,' Errol said. 'We are interested in more than reefers. We're interested in a murder case. When this police officer intercepted you, you were coming from Kingsmead Hall, back to your parked car. Isn't that so?'

'Yes. There was nothing illegal about it.'

'Then why did you try to escape? Because you were carrying reefers?'

'No.'

'Why, then?'

'Because I didn't want to make trouble for someone else.'

'For Miss Caroline Falcon?'

Deluce shook his head.

Errol asked: 'Does that headshake mean that the answer is "No"?'

'It means we're not talking about Miss Falcon.'

'I see. Now we'll go back to the night of Sir Richard Falcon's murder. You have already made one statement about that, but it wasn't given under oath. You can change your story if you like. Were you anywhere around Kingsmead on the night of the murder?'

'What makes you suggest that I was?'

'Some very elusive person was seen around there, before Sir Richard was seen coming home. It could have been you, just leaving. I think you visited Kings-mead Hall that night. Now don't be in a hurry to deny that. Other people will be questioned.'

'You'll go after Caroline?'

'You may compel us to. This is a murder job, man.'

'Well, all right. I was at the Hall that night. But I know nothing about the murder.'

'You went to the Hall from the Paraguay Club?'

'Yes.'

'With Miss Caroline?'

'Yes.'

'What time?'

'Going up to midnight.'

'Did you see any other member of the family?'

'Only the dog.'

'You went into the house?'

'Yes.'

'What time did you leave?'

'Around one o'clock.'

'Did Miss Caroline come to the gate with you?'

'No. She was tired. I let myself out. She'd told me that the dog wouldn't bother me coming away from the house, but I didn't trust it. I borrowed a sword.'

'But the dog didn't bother you?'

'No. I never saw it. I left the sword in long grass at the entrance to the estate. I was going to phone Carol the day after, and tell her.'

'We found the sword. Would you have killed the dog with it?'

'No. I thought a sword might fend it off.'

'Did you see anybody in the village? Or anywhere around there?'

'No.'

'Did you see *anything at all* of Sir Richard Falcon?'

'No.'

'When you were at the Hall that night, whereabouts in the house were you?'

'Do I have to answer that?'

'You don't *have* to answer anything,' Errol said reluctantly. 'But all this is confidential, you know.'

'Confidential to who? Whom?'

'To our four selves and my superiors in the C.I.D.'

'Well, we were in Carol's bedroom.'

'I see. All right. We'll have to wait until these home-made cigarettes have been properly examined. But there's this Assault on Police.' Errol turned to P.C. Baines. 'Were you badly hurt?'

'No, Sergeant,' said Baines. 'If you want to drop that charge, it's all right with me. But if it turns out to be a narcotic job, I'll have to give evidence of arrest.'

'Sure. But no need to mention the odd thump. A brief struggle, you could say. Right, that's settled. Mr. Deluce, see we're not piling it on, but until I know what's in these home-made cigs, I'm afraid I shall have to detain you on suspicion, under the Dangerous Drugs Act, 1967.'

'You're going to lock me up?'

'Yes. I'll see that you get a good breakfast. I would like to have your permission to search your flat, as a matter of routine.'

'And if I don't give permission?'

'I shall have to get a warrant and make the search just the same.'

'All right. You have permission.'

'Very good. We don't use the cells at this station. If you'll just write your initials on these three cigarettes, we'll be on our way to Headquarters, where you'll be treated with kindness.'

Deluce had enough spirit to show a grin. 'Nice, kind coppers,' he said. 'You're bringing tears to my eyes.'

Detective Sergeant Errol was waiting for Martineau's arrival at his office at nine o'clock the following morning, and he had with him the typed reports and statements relating to Leo Deluce's arrest.

'What's all this?' the D.C.I. asked, when the documents were put on his desk.

'Kingsmead again, sir,' said Errol, and he briefly outlined the matter. He concluded: 'I have Deluce outside here, in case you want to talk to him. I thought I might take the reefers to the laboratory, and be back here in time for him to be charged and put on the court sheet. That is if they *are* reefers, and I don't see what else they can be.'

Martineau opened the gold cigarette case. He sniffed at the three suspect cigarettes, and said: 'I fancy I can smell cannabis resin. I'll keep Deluce in here until you come back for him. What about young Caroline? Has he had a chance to get her on the phone this morning and fix up a tale?'

'No chance. And anyway I happen to know that she doesn't have a phone in her bedroom. Or she didn't, the night of the murder. Even if Deluce persuaded one of the gaolers to ring her up, he could hardly wake up the whole household, trying to reach her in the night. I arranged for two men to be at the Hall at eight o'clock this morning, to get her story when she came down for breakfast.'

'And Deluce's flat?'

'He gave permission to search. We found nothing.'

'Very good, Sergeant. You think of everything. This reefer job is going to make a bit of a stink. Pop singer, and all that. But the girl won't be in it unless she talks herself into it. Last night, did Deluce look as if he was drugged?'

'I'm no expert, sir. He looked normal to me.'

'All right, off you go.'

Errol departed. Martineau perused the documents he had left. Then he had Deluce brought in. He gave the young man a civil greeting, and offered him a chair, and kept him waiting while he looked at some crime reports.

Eventually he made a neat stack of the reports, and pushed them aside. He offered Deluce a cigarette. 'Not reefers,' he said without a smile.

'I'm told there's not much harm in the odd one,' Deluce replied.

'There is if you're caught with it. The moral or medical aspect of cannabis is no concern of the police. Only the legal aspect.'

'Where are they now?'

'At the laboratory. It's highly probable you'll be up before the bench this morning. How will it affect your career, if you're convicted?'

'I don't know. It won't be so good if I'm sent down.'

'No. First offence, is it?'

'I've never been in a police court.'

'No? Well, you're a public figure. The papers will make a fuss.'

'Suppose I use my real name?'

'You will. But you're known. The papers will feature the name of Deluce.'

'Good publicity if I get off.'

'*If* you do. The best of luck to you. This isn't my case, you know. What *I'm* interested in is the source of the stuff. I was hoping you could tell us more about that.'

'The pusher, you mean? I wish I could. Those reefers came from a friend who is definitely not a pusher. I don't want to involve my friend in any sort of reprisals.'

'I see. But couldn't you give us a hint?'

'I told the detective as much as I could. A sergeant, is he?'

'Detective Sergeant Errol, a very smart man.'

'Yes. I thought so. He reckons to be easy with you, but he doesn't miss any moves.'

'He can't afford to. Neither can I. I want to find out how cannabis resin is getting into this city. Those cigarettes are not just rubbed-up marijuana. I smelt the resin, which is stronger. Hashish, that is. So your friend is one stage further into addiction already. Pretty soon hashish won't be enough for him. He'll be on L.S.D. 25, which can make him permanently insane, or methedrine, which will ruin his health. Then the next step will be heroin or cocaine, or both. Have you ever heard of a Speedball?'

'No, I never have.'

'It's a few grains of heroin and two or three of cocaine. When a person goes flying on that he doesn't live long, and he dies miserably. He becomes both physically and mentally dependent on the drug, and he won't accept substitutes. When he fails to get the stuff, he suffers terribly. You may think I'm building up a horror story, but it is a fact that nearly all the hard drug addicts in this country today were started on innocent-looking reefers.'

'It's a long way from reefers to heroin.'

'It's a surprisingly short distance. I'd like to know who brings them into this town.'

'I can't tell you, but I'll give you a tip. I *have* heard

mention of a Chinaman. The kids call him Bob Eye, but that's only their name for him. None of 'em seems to know his real name.'

'What's he like?'

'I have no idea. I don't know whether he's old or young. I don't know whether he lives around these parts, or just visits occasionally. He might be a seaman for all I know.'

'Well, that's better than nothing. Thanks. Nobody will ever know that you told me.'

'I hope not. There's a name for people who tip off the police.'

'You need never be ashamed of shopping a filthy drug pusher. It's kids who fall for it, you know. Just when they're at the right age to be ruined for life. You know the dangers of having one addict in a crowd of youngsters? He wants all the others to share his experiences. He's a salesman for the real salesman. That's why I think all addicts should be locked up.'

'Will *I* be locked up? That's what is bothering me.'

'I don't know. There'll be a remand for the completion of inquiries. You *should* get bail.'

There was a knock on the door. Errol entered. He looked at Martineau and nodded significantly. Then he said to Deluce: 'Come along, young man.'

Errol took Deluce to the charge room. Martineau spoke to Detective Superintendent Clay on the intercom. He said: 'Leo Deluce is now being charged with the illegal possession of cannabis resin. There'll probably be a remand. I suggest that the police don't oppose bail, sir. Deluce is no good to me in a cell.'

'We won't oppose bail. I'll see to it.'

In the presence of her mother, and apparently without being too shamefaced, Caroline Falcon corroborated Leo Deluce's story about his visits to her room. But she denied any knowledge that he had been in possession of cannabis—translated to her as reefers—and that he had ever smoked any in her presence. She invited the police to search her room, an offer which they immediately accepted. There were half-full bottles of whisky, gin, vermouth and Campari. There was no cannabis and no odour of it.

The officers reported that Lady Falcon made not a word of comment during the interview. Also, both officers were of the opinion that she had been neither greatly shocked nor greatly worried. They were sensible men with much experience of dealing with people in trouble, and Chief Inspector Martineau accepted their impressions as accurate.

He thought that Lady Falcon's lack of reaction was rather strange. Well, she had had enough trouble recently. Perhaps she was getting used to it.

11

Salvador Segura was stringing an old guitar he had bought when Manuel Dominguez called at the caravan encampment.

'*Boona dia*, Manolo,' he said, and that was Andaluz for '*Buenos dias*'.

'*Dia*,' said Manolo, even more curtly, and the boy Jose, frowning over an English-Spanish book, looked up and said '*Dia*'. The girl Conchita gave the visitor a flashing smile, and said nothing.

Manolo found a seat, lit a cigarette, and remarked

that the weather was good. Salvador agreed. Jose had returned to his book.

There was silence. Manolo looked at Conchita over the heads of her father and brother. The reply to his glance was a very slight and secret shake of the head. He began to watch Salvador at his task.

Salvador worked in leisurely fashion, but his long, strong fingers were nimble. He was a very quiet man and, Manolo knew, very dangerous. He was as expert with his *cuchillo* as he was with his guitar, but since the arrival in England there had seemed to be nothing to fight about.

There might be soon, Manolo thought. He took a deep breath, and said formally: 'I am rich enough to marry your daughter, Concepcion.'

Salvador did not laugh at the proposal, nor did he look at the proposer. His glance flicked once at Conchita, and he saw that she was wide-eyed, looking slightly alarmed. The boy Jose was looking narrow-eyed at Manolo, apparently ready for trouble. The father was unconcerned. Both his children enjoyed putting on an act.

'I am glad you are rich, Manolo,' he said. 'And you are also a fine young man. But you cannot marry Concepcion this year, nor maybe next year. We are making too much money with the night club.'

'But I really am rich,' Manolo persisted. 'And the night club is only for the time being.'

'The time being might be a long time. A man has been to see me about a disco.'

'They cannot make a disco of the dance.'

'No. Of the singing, and the guitar, and the castanets.'

Manolo was silent then, because he also was a taciturn man. He brooded. Perhaps the Segura family were

going to be rich, *really* rich like film stars. They we:
good performers, he knew. The best of all the gypsi
in Andalusia. It had only been the jealousy of tl
powerful and numerous Miguelin family of dance
which had prevented them from being rich even i
Spain. They would do well in England.

Salvador and his children remained silent, wise.
giving Manolo time to think it over. But Manolo w;
thinking of the past. His father had been Salvador
godfather, and when he was born Salvador had swoi
to be an elder brother to him. But in those days Salv;
dor's guitar could earn him no more than a few be;
garly centimos, and he had made his living the tru
gypsy way. And this way he had faithfully taugl
Manolo: to poach, to cheat, to steal.

In those days the Andalusian coast was und
veloped. The few Britishers who had discovered th
advantages of sojourning in or around Malaga ha
wisely kept quiet about it, and many of them had bee
able to live there like Sahibs on their small pension:
Then, through the newspapers, the Americans an
northern Europeans began to be aware of holida
places they had never heard of before. The Malag
coast became the Costa del Sol. People went there an
returned home raving about the cheapness of ever}
thing. In the 1950's the real exploitation began. Th
tall hotels began to go up, and up and up, from Gibra
tar to Malaga, and then from Alicante to the north c
Barcelona.

This development was a bonanza for the Segura an
Dominguez families. As a slender lad of ten, Manol
learned to slip his greased body through opening
which did not look big enough for a cat. He had passe(
out money, jewelry, watches, clothes, and anythin

else he could lay his hands on. Those had been pros-
perous days, until one still, hot night when he had
entered the ground-floor bedroom of a tall Dane. It
was expected that a man on holiday would be affected
by liquor, and sleeping heavily, and it was the intention to take everything he had except the pyjamas he
wore. But the man woke up, and lay still until the boy
came within his reach. Then he slipped out of bed and
laid a big hand on a slippery shoulder. The boy twisted
away in a fright, and when he was grasped again he
used his knife. As it happened, the Dane had been
sleeping naked, and the thin sharp blade of the knife
slipped easily into his heart.

The boy Manolo knew where that upward thrust
had gone. He heard the thud as the man fell, and after
that there was neither sound nor movement. Petrified
with fear, he stood still, listening for an alarm. Salvador's hoarse whisper from the window set him in mo-
tion. He got out of there at once. He showed his knife
and spoke of death, and the gypsies fled.

It took them an hour to reach their encampment.
The women and then the children were quietly awakened. They struck their shabby tents and packed their
few possessions. Without waiting for morning they
loaded their two *burros* and headed deeper into the
hills. They travelled with all speed until they were far
away in the fastnesses of the Sierra Moreno.

On the journey they got rid of evidence. Manolo's
knife and the Dane's clothes were dropped here and
there into rapid streams. The man's gold watch was
buried, and only his money was kept. The gypsies knew
that the sudden flight of two families would be noted
by the *Guardia Civile*. There would be a hunt for
them. The Segura-Dominguez clan fled further and

further north. It was fortunate for them that they had a considerable amount of stolen money.

They journeyed into a lonely life. In central and northern Spain they were outcasts, even among other gypsies. Nobody wanted them. The *Guardia* harassed them, but they used false names and avoided suspicion of the murder of the Dane. Their story was that they were making for Barcelona, where they had family connections. There had to be some explanation as to how Andalusian gypsies could be so far north.

They found that Barcelona was richer than the cities of Andalusia. It was richer even than Seville. Salvador did better with his guitar, and his daughter Conchita was developing a pleasing voice. And even as a child she danced well. The *flamenco* she performed was not native to Barcelona. The Segura family began to make a modest living.

Three years passed. Conchita's mother died. Her brother Jose began to show that he also could dance. Manolo was taller and broader, and after being scrubbed and dressed for the occasion he got a summertime job as a kitchen boy in a hotel. It was promised that if he worked well he would have the chance to learn to be a waiter.

The winters of northern Spain can be severe, especially for people living in primitive conditions. Salvador and his two children found rooms in Barcelona, but the Dominguez family stayed in the tents. Manolo's father died of pneumonia, and his mother had a fatal heart attack through struggling up and down snow-covered slopes looking for firewood. Manolo sold the donkeys, and moved in with Salvador and family.

Two years later young Jose's voice cracked and broke, and his father realised that he too would be a singer. Jose and Conchita began to sing naturally in harmony. At seventeen Manolo had a deep voice, but there was no music in it. But he was now a regular junior waiter. Whether or not he was jealous of Jose, he held his peace and applied himself to his work. Physically, he was a fine stripling; tall, broad, and strong. Like every young Spaniard of good physique, he sometimes dreamed of being a *torero*, and possibly even a *matador*.

The gypsy life was now only a memory, and not a pleasant one. Salvador decided to go back to the south, by stages: Tarragona, Valencia, Alicante, Malaga. Malaga was the city and port of the Costa del Sol. He knew it well. Living as a townsman and not as a gypsy, he thought he would now be safe there. The Costa del Sol was now thick with night clubs and other places of entertainment, he had heard. The subsidiary holiday resorts were strung like lanterns along the coast: Torremolinos, Fuengirola, Marbella, and a host of smaller places. And the season was all the year round.

Manolo, with a good reference from his employer, decided that he also would go south. They all went by bus, from town to town. It was the end of the season on the Costa Brava, and hotels and clubs were closing for the winter. They found no work until they reached Benedorm. The work there was not very satisfactory to Salvador, so they went on, to the southernmost city, Malaga.

Malaga was virtually unchanged, but Torremolinos, a few kilometres along the coast, was transformed. It was crowded with Americans, British, Germans, Scandinavians and French. There were a number of French restaurants, bars, and night clubs. The tall new hotels stood in line for miles. Salvador was impressed.

He remembered the place when it was little more than a fishing village.

In Torremolinos they all did well, and Salvador even became the owner of a roadworthy car, which Manolo learned to drive. Time went by. Both Manolo and Jose went to do their military service. Conchita had suitors, but they were not the sort who wished to marry her, and she spurned them. The boys returned, young men now, though Manolo was the older, and looked it. Both Jose and Conchita had fine voices now, and their harmony was faultless. Salvador developed the act until it was very good indeed, and the family group became locally famous.

In years they had met no one who seemed to know them, but inevitably one night during their performance a captain of the *Guardia Civile* walked into the club and showed great interest in Salvador. Salvador also remembered him, and he was afraid. After the act, the Guardia captain went to talk to the club manager. That was enough for Salvador. Neither he nor his children went to their dressing rooms. They walked straight out of the club.

Manolo was working as a waiter in a nearby hotel. Jose went for him. He walked away from the table he was serving. At home, Conchita, Jose and Manolo changed into their oldest clothes, and packed what they could carry. Meanwhile Salvador was in a bar, trading his car for two good donkeys. They went away from Torremolinos, and spent the night in the hills.

In the morning, as soon as the banks were open, Salvador ventured into Torremolinos and withdrew his money—a considerable amount—from the Banco de Viscaya. Manolo's small savings were not disturbed. During that day, in the back streets of Malaga, all the time in fear of recognition by a policeman, he purchased the second-hand tents and equipment he required. The donkeys were loaded, and the Segura family, gypsies once again, headed for the sierras. And winter was approaching.

They reached Madrid, and felt safer there. But they had had to change the name of their act, and there was no work for them. Manolo had known a few young Spaniards who had gone to work as waiters in England. He mentioned this, and Salvador also considered England.

'We need passports,' he said. 'In Barcelona we will get passports.'

To Barcelona they went, and by clever evasion and some bribery they secured passports without disclosing their true identities. They also got from the British consul permits to work in England. All this took time. It was spring again before they flew to England.

In England, unable to speak the language, they were like bewildered children. But people were helpful, and a surprising number of them could speak a little Spanish. The three younger people picked up the language fairly quickly. Manolo worked as a waiter, Jose worked as a labourer on a road gang, and eventually Conchita was able to work as a waitress. Salvador haunted the better-class bars of London in the hope of meeting a Spaniard who could give him the sort of information he wanted.

At last he met a Spanish barman who had been ten years in England. He happened to know a theatrical agent. He introduced Salvador to the man, and acted as interpreter. An audition was arranged easily enough, because the man was not a very eminent agent.

'Very good,' he said after the audition. 'But I'm

blessed if I know where I can fit you in.' He sat in thought, and had an idea. 'A circus any good?'

Salvador's friend translated. Salvador did not see much future in a circus. He smiled and shrugged, but he said: 'Possibly.' In Spanish the word is pronounced 'Posseeblay'.

The agent became busy on the telephone, with the proprietor of a small circus.

'Spanish dancing,' the agent said. 'A beautiful girl. Flamenco, it is.'

'H'm,' said the circus man. 'I've never had a dancing act before. I could try it. We can't do worse than we are doing.'

The terms he offered were low. But at least they were a start in England. Salvador accepted.

The agent was something of a hypocrite. 'You'll never regret it,' he said heartily. 'I'll make out a contract.'

Since neither Salvador nor his friend could read English, the contract was not signed until it had been seen by an English solicitor. He perused it and commented: 'This just about ties you up for life.'

'I want only for the circus,' said Salvador, and the contract was amended on those lines.

The circus was at Oxford. Salvador and family were allotted a comfortable caravan. They found life bearable, and they made friends with Jesse Smith the gypsy. Out of his memories of childhood Salvador dredged certain Romany words which were understood by Jesse. He was intrigued by this meeting with Spanish gypsies, and he was very helpful when the circus proprietor went bankrupt six months later. With their pay in arrears, the two gypsy families found themselves in possession of horses, caravans, and a Land

Rover. They spent a quiet winter moving from place to place, earning a few pounds here and there. In early spring they found a good camping site on the edge of the moors above Granchester. They settled there with the intention of staying for some time.

In London, Manolo had missed his old friends. Especially had he missed Conchita. He was in love with her. He did not know if she was in love with him. She had met him secretly a few times. They had made love after a fashion, but she had permitted no real intimacy.

When he learned about the new camp site, Manolo moved to Granchester. He found work with a very profitable sideline. He was twenty-five years old, and he had money. He wanted to marry Conchita, and here was Salvador being difficult about it. Seemingly he had forgotten that he had once sworn to be Manolo's god-brother.

Having thought at great length about the past, Manolo rose to his feet. Father and son looked directly at him, somewhat in surprise. He looked at Conchita, but she pretended to be looking for something in a cupboard.

'Well, we shall see,' he said. He turned, to depart. '*Adios*,' he said.

'*Adios*, Manolo,' all three of them said. Conchita was only a little worried. Salvador and Jose were not at all worried about Manolo. Things were going well with them. What was there to worry about?

Come death and death duties, the Falcon business had
to go on. Young Peter Falcon moved from Falcon
Motors, his uncle's concern, to Falcon Machine Tools:
in stock-exchange parlance, from F.M. to F.M.T.
Peter was not immediately made a director, but it was
understood that he soon would be. His mother, sister
and himself now owned a majority of the F.M.T.
shares, because Sir Richard had always been firmly in
control of his own business. Now it appeared that Peter
also would be in control in due time. Of that family
majority of shares, the largest portion was his. The like-
able, carefree youth had become an important man.

The change of fortune did not change Peter. It did
not seem that he would have to buy a larger size in
hats. He was now head of his own branch of the family,
but he did not seek to show his authority. It was not
expected that a young man of his type would be en-
thusiastic about any sort of acquaintance with the
Seven Foot Four, but he did not interfere with the
friendship of Leo Deluce and Caroline. Perhaps, some
people thought, he was playing a waiting game. Perhaps he was waiting for the Falcon murder case to be
settled, and for public interest in the family to die
down.

Naturally it was expected that Peter would transfer
his Rugby football enthusiasm from Yoreborough to
his own home town. He had plenty of friends of his
own age in Granchester, and he was the sort of man
the Granchester R.U.F.C. needed. Already, after a decent interval of a few days, friends were seeking him

out. The Honourable Lawrence Geever was one of these. They had been friends from childhood.

Larry took Peter around. They went to see the floor show at the Paraguay Club, and Peter refused to be impressed by the Seven Foot Four. Another time they went to the Tahiti Club, and Larry said: 'Just wait till you see this Spanish dancer.'

Peter saw the dancer, and the dancer saw Peter. He and Larry had a ringside table, and the dancer had a number which entailed the use of a sort of scarf or small shawl. At the end of the dance the scarf landed at Peter's feet. He stared in astonishment as the girl disappeared behind the curtain which was the way to the dressing rooms, then he picked up the scarf and followed her. There was some laughter and a buzz of interested comment from people at other tables. Salvador Segura put down his guitar, and his son Jose looked a question at him.

The club manager was beside them in a moment. 'Steady,' he said with one hand on Salvador's shoulder and the other on Jose's elbow. 'That is *Sir* Peter Falcon.'

'He is a Sir? Like a marquis?'

'Something like that. He is very rich. Millions, he has. Millions of pounds, not pesetas.'

A nobleman with a million pounds! Salvador picked up his guitar.

Behind the curtain there was a pleasant if halting conversation for five minutes. Nothing of importance was said, but Peter was captivated by the Spanish girl's sparkle, and by her intriguing accent as she tried to speak English. He learned her name. Conchita! That was really romantic. When she heard his name she laughed, and called him Pedro. That amused him.

When at last the girl excused herself, he returned beaming to his table.

'You dog!' said Larry in envious admiration. 'You're just back in time. Her old man and her brother were getting ready to knife you.'

Peter looked at the guitarist in surprise. Salvador smiled gravely and inclined his head. Peter also smiled, and bowed in return. Jose was expressionless during this exchange.

The following night Peter went alone to the Tahiti Club. His arrival was preceded by a uniformed florist's messenger, who carried a huge bouquet of flowers to Conchita's dressing room.

When Peter was at his table, Conchita came out to him, to thank him for the flowers. He invited her to sit with him.

'Dos minutos,' she said as she accepted. 'I must not remain. *Gracias*, no, I will not drink.'

She accepted a cigarette, and looked at him mischievously through the smoke. She said: 'I learn that you are a noche.'

He grinned back at her. 'What is a noche?'

'A night, is it not?'

He laughed. 'A night on the tiles? Or a knight in armour? I'm not a knight. I'm a baronet.'

'And what is that?'

'A knight with hereditary trimmings.'

Obviously that sort of English was incomprehensible to her. 'You are Sirr Pedro de Falco,' she said firmly.

'I'm a knight whose father won his spurs for him. Call me Pete.'

'Pete?' She frowned. 'Peterr I like better. Sirr Peterr.' She laughed then. Charmed by her, he joined in the laughter.

There was not much they could talk about, but the mood was excellent. He took a small book from his pocket, and showed it to her. He had learned a few words. He said '*Amor*' and '*Inamorata*'.

She pretended hauteur. '*Bastante*,' she said.

'What does that mean?'

'It means "eenough",' she said curtly, and then her hauteur broke down into laughter.

The boy Jose appeared at the curtain. He looked at his sister, and then made a show of looking at his watch.

'I go,' she said, rising. '*Adios, amigo*.'

'*Adios, Querida*,' he replied.

Again she tried to look haughty. He watched her as she moved away. At the curtain she turned and smiled.

When the Segura act appeared, Conchita danced for Peter as if he were a sultan and she a slave girl. He was too enthralled to be embarrassed.

He had it bad. He admitted it to himself. But mentally he shied away from the question of what might happen, because it had not really started yet. Young men of his sort were apt to divide girls into two kinds; those to have fun with and those who might be suitable for marriage. Conchita he regarded as fun, and anyway he did not yet feel ready for marriage.

Salvador Segura was not displeased by the way things were going between his daughter and the rich English Sir. On Sunday morning he had arrived at the caravan to take out Conchita for the day, not in his vintage Bentley but in the splendid Rolls-Royce which had been his father's. 'A million pesetas,' had been Salvador's thought when he saw the car. Undoubtedly the Sir was rich.

The Sir and the *señorita* rode away over the moors in the million-peseta car, and they would not be back until the evening. And in the afternoon Manuel Dominguez appeared. He found a seat, lit a cigarette, and gossiped for a while. Then he asked where Conchita might be.

'She is away for a little while,' said Salvador, and young Jose chuckled.

The visitor's glance flicked once towards Jose, then returned to Salvador. 'Away where?' he asked, as if the answer would be of no importance.

'On private business, Manolo,' said Salvador firmly. He was being careful. Manolo had shown a serious interest in Conchita, and he was a man capable of violence. It would certainly have been unwise to tell him about the English Sir.

'Who is escorting her?' Manolo persisted languidly.

'In Inglaterra she is old enough to go without escort.'

'Ah,' said Manolo, and that was all. He stayed for an hour and was given a drink of whisky. When the subject of Conchita had been dropped, Salvador was friendly enough, though Jose sulked as he usually did when Manolo was present. But it became evident to the visitor that he was not going to be asked to stay for a meal. Such uncharacteristic lack of hospitality made him suspect that Salvador did not want him to be around when Conchita returned from her so-private business trip. He departed, apparently going away to Granchester.

He did not go as far as the culvert where he had once hidden some stolen jewelry. He had recently called there in the dead of night and had found no jewelry there. He had wondered about that, but now he thought of Jose Segura, who had been so amused because Conchita was away. Jose should have been his friend, but never had been. From childhood days Jose had been jealous of every mouthful which the stronger Manolo ate. Had Jose somehow found the jewels? That might never be known, but it was known that he had laughed maliciously when Conchita's absence had been mentioned. It would please him to see his old playmate forgotten by Conchita, discarded for an English *novio*. Was that the case, then?

Manolo sat on a grassy bank and counted his cigarettes. He had enough. He knew that he might have a long time to wait, but he would not be too hungry so long as he had cigarettes. He went in search of a place from which he could watch in concealment.

The sun was behind a hill when he saw the Rolls come down the road to the caravan site. He was amazed that such a car should stop there. It was still light enough for him to see the young man who alighted. This man ran round the car and opened the door for Conchita. He might have embraced her there, but laughingly she avoided him. She ran to the caravan and waved from there. He stood for a moment after she had gone inside, then he got into the car and drove away.

Quietly Manolo said some hard things about Conchita, whom he had regarded as his sweetheart. He crouched there, deep in thought. The Tahiti Club, he decided. Conchita had met the man there. He would go there to watch her dance. He could be watched, followed, and identified.

Manolo had money. He judged that he could stay around this neighbourhood until the matter of Conchita and her *novio* had been settled to his own satisfaction. He realised that now it might be dangerous for him to report as an alien at a police station. That meant that the police would soon be seeking him for failing to report. Well, he would just have to be careful and keep out of the way of policemen.

The Dog Man still continued his career of burglary, and the Granchester police still made every effort to find him. They also impressed their need upon the police of neighbouring boroughs, and upon the police of three adjacent counties. When the proposed amalgamations became reality, the borough forces would be merged with the counties, and then in that region there would be only five police forces: two big cities and three counties. And even then the Granchester C.I.D. men doubted if they would get the sort of help they wanted from police forces who were not concerned about the Dog Man.

Besides the Dog Man there was the Falcon murder job. That seemed to be at a standstill. There was one main suspect and he was the Dog Man, and he could not be found. Detective Chief Inspector Martineau was as frustrated as ever he had been. Neither publicity nor ceaseless inquiry nor unremitting vigilance seemed to be of any use. So called 'information' poured into the C.I.D. by letter, telephone, and word of mouth. Every one of these 'tips' was investigated. None of them was even promising. As Superintendent Clay complained, there wasn't even anything to feel hopeful about.

The fine weather continued: sunny days and lovely still nights. The Dog Man grew somewhat richer and a number of insurance companies grew slightly poorer. Policemen on night duty did not lose their strong desire to make contact with the Dog Man, and they asked each other irritably how the devil he managed to move around without being seen.

Observations made it clear that Leo Deluce's nocturnal visits to Kingsmead Hall had ceased, at least for the time being. Kingsmead village was its normal sleepy self again, but P.C. Baines did not lose the feeling that something else would happen at the Hall. When he was on nights he never failed to ride up to the gates and have a chat with the dog Rajah, and Rajah showed no signs of liking him any better for it.

At the end of his short remand, Leo Deluce appeared before a Stipendiary Magistrate, charged with being in possession of a quantity of cannabis resin. He had no previous convictions of any sort, and his lawyer told the very thin story that someone must have put the reefers into his cigarette case for a joke. Leo also maintained that he had not tried to smoke one. Whether or not his tale was believed, the magistrate fined him £50 and let him go. The newspapers played up the case because he was a pop singer, and most of them displayed a picture of him walking away from the police court with Caroline Falcon on his arm.

All the members of the Falcon family and household were to some extent under police observation, and so to a smaller extent were all the people known to have even a slight connection with the Falcon murder. Such was the hunt for even the slightest clue that a copy of every sort of report about dogs was sent into the C.I.D. and detectives were instructed to cut out every newspaper story or article about dogs and put it on a tray on the main desk in the C.I.D. office. Both Martineau and Clay perused these cuttings and reports regularly and religiously. Both were convinced of the importance of dogs, even in the Falcon murder case.

One moonlight night, a little after midnight, P.C. Baines thought he had got something. As he pottered quietly on his motor-cycle up the drive towards Kingsmead Hall, he discerned the figure of a man beside the field gate which Leo Deluce had used the night he was caught there. The man was moving away across the field. Baines turned around and went back to Kingsmead village, and through the village to the city boundary. There he stopped his machine and went on foot, hoping to be in time to meet the man as he emerged by the other gate into Kingsmead Wood.

He was in time. He met the man within a few yards of the place where he had met Leo Deluce. The man did not try to run away. He faced the policeman, but his attitude suggested that he was ready for action.

'Now then,' said Baines, also ready. 'What are you doing here at this time of night?'

The stranger smiled, and made a gesture indicating helplessness. There was moonlight at that spot among the trees and Baines noticed that he was young, in his twenties, and a right handy-looking lad. He was big, and he looked quick and strong. His dark clothes were of a workman's type: overalls and a donkey jacket. He was hatless, and his hair was dark and coarse-looking. He had the look of an outdoors man.

'I asked you something,' said Baines. 'I want an answer.'

The man opened his mouth and tapped his lower lip with a forefinger. Then he tapped one of his ears. He appeared to try to say something. It was something between a moan and a grunt. Then he dropped his hands to his side and shrugged.

'Oh,' said Baines. 'So you're reckoning to be a

dummy, are you? That deaf-and-dumb stunt is as old as my grandmother.'

The man looked mildly puzzled. He shrugged again. Baines made a movement of his hands, suggesting that the man should turn around. The man understood, and he obeyed without hesitation. Baines went closer and tapped pockets. He convinced himself that this fellow was carrying neither weapons nor housebreaking tools. There was not even a glass-cutter or a penknife. But he was wearing gloves. He did not look the sort who would wear gloves on a summer's night.

Baines took him by the arm. 'Come along,' he said. 'We'll see if we can find out who you are.'

Together they walked to Baines's motor-cycle. Baines wondered if he ought to call up a car, or if he could risk taking the man in on his pillion seat. He decided to take the risk. He got astride the machine, started it up. and pointed to the pillion seat. The man straddled the seat with apparent willingness.

They rode to Westholme police station, D Division, without incident. In the C.I.D., Detective Sergeant Errol and Detective Constable Cooper were present. They looked at Baines's captive with interest, having the Dog Man in mind.

Baines understood. 'Yeh, he looks the part,' he said. 'But he don't seem to have a damned thing on him.'

'Where did you pick him up?'

'Same place as I got Leo Deluce. I first saw him going across the field, away from Kingsmead Hall. I nipped round by the road and intercepted. He seems quiet enough. Too quiet, in fact.'

'What's your name?' Errol asked the prisoner. The man merely stared at him.

'He makes out he's deaf and dumb,' Baines volunteered. 'Not a word for the cat.'

'Empty his pockets.'

Baines and Cooper obeyed the order. They found cigarettes, matches, and handkerchief, a peculiar object wrapped in cellophane, two keys and about ten shillings in change. There was nothing else.

Errol unwrapped the cellophane. 'What's this?' he demanded, and nobody answered.

The object appeared to be a dried and withered human thumb. Errol sniffed at it. There was a faint, unpleasant smell. 'Well, that's one for the museum,' he said, as he rewrapped the object and put it on the desk. The prisoner immediately reached for it and replaced it in his pocket.

'It's his lucky charm,' Cooper guessed, with a grin.

They allowed the man to keep his grisly relic, and tried to trick him into talking. They also tried to make him fall into the trap of showing that he could hear what was being said. They discussed him openly in the most insulting terms they could give utterance to, but the man gave no sign of understanding. When Errol lit a cigarette the prisoner reached for his own. He lit a cigarette and put cigarettes and matches in his pocket. When nobody objected he picked up the rest of his property and pocketed that also.

'Well, what are we going to do with him?' Errol asked eventually. 'He wasn't even on enclosed premises.'

'If he saw me, or heard my motor-bike, he could have dumped his glass-cutter and stuff while he was crossing the field,' Baines suggested.

Since there looked as if there might be a discussion, the prisoner retired a step or two and quietly sat down on a chair beside the wall of the room.

'We should hold him till we've searched that field in daylight,' Errol said. 'In any case I might get my head in my hands if I don't let Martineau see him and his dried thumb.'

He tried a last trick. He turned, with his hand out. 'Let me look at that thumb again.'

The prisoner was not taken by surprise. He looked puzzled, and then offered his matches.

Errol pushed the matches back into the man's pocket and found the thumb again. He unwrapped it and put it on the desk. All three policemen looked at it. Baines and Cooper stooped to sniff at it.

'It's a grim sort of luck piece,' Baines commented.

He turned to the prisoner in time to see him drifting quietly out through the open doorway of the C.I.D. office. He said 'Oy!' and gave chase, followed by his two colleagues.

The prisoner had fled silently down the short corridor, and was pushing open the swing door leading to the small entrance hall. By the time Baines was in the entrance hall, the only sign of the prisoner was the outer door swinging gently.

Westholme police station is on a hill. Baines's motor-cycle was at the kerb, facing downhill. Baines was in time to see his captive running with the machine, pushing it to gain speed. As it did gather speed he mounted it and coasted down the hill.

Baines pelted after him. At first he gained on the man, but as the slope of the hill increased he was left behind. But he kept on running. If this dummy did not know how to handle a motor-bike, he could still be kept in sight after he reached the bottom of the hill.

The hill eased gently off to level ground, and even

then the motor-cycle rolled for some distance at a good speed. Baines kept it in sight, but he realised that he would soon be weary. Then Errol and Cooper came down the hill in a C.I.D. car. They did not stop to pick up Baines, but went headlong after the motor-cycle.

The so-called dummy must at least not have been deaf. Obviously he heard the car in the quietness of the night. He stopped, and abandoned the motor-cycle near the bridge over the Holme Brook. Right there beside him were the few steps down on to the path along the riverside. He took the steps in one, and ran along the path. By the time Errol and Cooper had arrived and alighted, he was out of sight. He was running into an area of suburban development, with many walls and hedges for cover. Beyond this built-up area there were woods and fields.

The policemen searched for the 'dummy', and then put out the word for him by radio. But they did not see him again that night.

13

P.C. Baines was on duty until six in the morning, so he did not mind spending the daylight hours from three to six searching a field. Errol and Cooper had been officially on duty until two in the morning, but they were C.I.D. men who knew that they had been guilty of negligence. They also searched from three until six, and if either of them were disgruntled about that, it was silent disgruntlement.

Baines and Errol submitted their reports before they went home to bed, but at two o'clock in the afternoon both of them were in Martineau's office. Both of them were somewhat apprehensive, and they had need to be. They were in danger of disciplinary action for neglect of duty. They had allowed a prisoner to escape. Though at the time the man had been no more than a suspect, still he had escaped before the inquiry into his antecedents had been completed.

Martineau's curt greeting did not make them any happier. Before him on his desk he had their reports, and he also had the grisly relic wrapped in cellophane.

'You did right well,' he said. 'This deaf-and-dumb character you had was undoubtedly a thief, and he might have been the Dog Man. So you had to let him slip you.'

Baines, the constable, remained silent. Errol, the detective sergeant, required some qualifications of the phrase 'undoubtedly a thief'. He asked: 'Have you got additional evidence, sir?'

'No. No more than you had.' Martineau unrolled the cellophane. 'Do you know what this is?'

'A mummified thumb, I suppose.'

'Did you ever read Dr. Hans Gross, on the superstitions of criminals?'

'Er, no, sir.'

'This is a slumber thumb. Supposedly the left thumb of a corpse nine weeks in the grave and temporarily disinterred under a new moon. It's all silly superstition, of course, but the thief who carries it believes it prevents people from waking up while he's robbing the house. In France it is called a *"main de gloire"*. Don't ask me why.'

'I thought that kind of thing had gone out of existence.'

'In this country, I daresay. But how about central

and eastern Europe? And Italy and Spain? I think plenty of ancient superstitions survive there. Do you know what is important about the slumber thumb?'

'No, sir.'

'According to Hans Gross, it is used only by gypsies. You say this dummy you had was about twenty-five years old. In that case he probably inherited this thing from his father or uncle. He's a gypsy. Did he look like one?'

'He was dark enough,' Errol admitted.

'Very coarse black hair,' said Baines. 'He could have been a gypsy, all right.'

'Didn't he utter any word or phrase at all?'

'He reckoned to try and talk to me,' said Baines. 'It was nothing but "Ooh ooh" and "Ah Ah".'

'Perhaps he feigned dumbness because his English wasn't so good?'

'Happen so, sir.'

'He's a gypsy, and probably not an English one. He might be an Irish gypsy, with an accent he doesn't want to advertise. Or he might be from some part of Europe. The slumber thumb makes that more likely.'

'I'll have to go to work on gypsies, sir,' said Errol, his use of the singular pronoun suggesting that he was willing to work harder after his lapse.

'We'll all have to do that. And I hope somebody can get hold of the Dog Man without managing to let him go.'

Martineau then went on to speak of immediate tasks, without so much as mentioning the Discipline Code. The two men from D Division carefully concealed their relief. They tried to make intelligent suggestions, to keep Martineau's mind well away from discipline. Errol thought that a more thorough search of the field for housebreaking tools would be a good idea. Baines wondered if inquiries at Kingsmead Hall would be of any help.

'You both think you're getting away with something, don't you?' said Martineau grimly.

That was a question to which Yes or No could be an unfortunate answer. Neither man tried to answer.

'All right,' said Martineau. 'You're both getting away with it because you've done your best on the big job. Baines has done particularly well, since he did not have the opportunities of a C.I.D. man. But don't think I'm giving either of you any medals. I'm permitting no more mistakes to go unpunished. Remember that.'

'Only your own,' said Baines ungratefully, but he said it to himself. It was an axiom in the lower ranks that only the bosses could cover their mistakes.

Martineau knew quite well what was said in the lower ranks, and he had a good idea of what Baines was thinking. But he did not give it a thought. Let them think what they liked. He proceeded to give instructions about searches, about interviews, about the search of records and perusal of photographs, and about Identikit.

'Now then,' he said finally. 'That should keep us all busy. And I only hope the Dog Man comes to claim his hereditary thumb.'

Martineau decided to visit Kingsmead Hall himself, and instead of taking his usual aide, Devery, he took Errol. He did not telephone to make an appointment. He decided to take a chance on the dog being loose, for the sake of arriving unannounced.

He and his companion arrived at the gates of the Hall at about ten minutes past three, and they were reassured by seeing Fletcher the chauffeur emerging, taking the dog for a walk. On the lead, and muzzled, Rajah was quiet. Perhaps he understood the meaning of the muzzle, because he ignored the two men in the C.I.D. car. Fletcher opened the gate for them and they drove up to the house. A silver-grey Rolls-Royce was waiting at the door. Brandon the butler met them there. Martineau could have started his inquiry by questioning the man, but he thought that it would be courteous to speak to Lady Falcon first. He asked to see her and was bidden to wait a moment. The butler went into the hall-cum-lounge, and returned almost at once.

'Will you please come this way, sir?' he said.

Lady Falcon was in the lounge with Lord Geever.

'Good afternoon, Inspector,' the lady said. 'Have you news for me?'

'Not really news,' Martineau told her. 'But I would like a quiet word with you.'

Geever did not seem to be at all pleased by the arrival of the detectives, but apparently he had no intention of letting them drive him away altogether. 'I'll take a turn on the terrace,' he said, rising and walking out.

But seemingly the interruption had not displeased Lady Falcon. She smiled as she said: 'Do sit down, both of you. And tell me what I can do for you.'

'If I get any help, it's more likely to be from one of your staff, your Ladyship. But it seemed right to come to you first. One of my men intercepted a—a prowler last night. Either he had been here, or he was on his way here.'

'Oh dear. What time would that be?'

'A little after midnight. He ran away across the field

when he saw the policeman, and he was caught in Kingsmead Wood. We believe he was a gypsy. Have you had any gypsies around here at all?'

'Not to my knowledge, Inspector. Fletcher the chauffeur, or somebody in the village, is more likely to be able to tell you about that.'

'Are there any deaf-and-dumb people in the village?'

'If there are, they're visitors.'

'I suppose everyone here was in bed by midnight?'

'No. *I* was up. And neither Peter nor Caroline had come in.'

'Were you alone?'

'Oh, I was safe enough. I had the dog with me.'

'Did he give signs of hearing anyone?'

'No. He was sitting here on the hearth, and he wasn't asleep. He's a real night owl, you know. He was wide awake, ready to go out.'

'Was any other member of the household still awake?'

'I don't think so. Brandon had gone to bed. When he told me he was going, he said everyone else was upstairs. That's why I kept the dog with me. I waited until Caroline came in about half-past twelve. Then we let Rajah out and went up to bed. I don't know what time Peter came home. He seems to be going to night clubs.'

'Did Miss Caroline come home alone?'

'Yes. What . . . ? Oh, I see. You're thinking the prowler might have been lying in wait. Well, I suppose you've got him under lock and key now.'

'No, my Lady. He escaped.'

'Oh.' Lady Falcon was perturbed. 'I shall have to tell Caroline not to come home alone.'

'It would be as well, perhaps. For a time. The

117

prowler was a young, strong man. He was deaf-and-dumb, or he pretended to be. That always gives the impression of a backward mentality, though it is usually a wrong impression. I suggest that both yourself and Miss Caroline take normal precautions.'

'Yes, of course. Thank you, Inspector.'

'Has there been any alarm or disturbance at all, during the past few days?'

'Not to my knowledge.'

'Thank you. Now I wonder if I could talk to Mr. Brandon.'

'Certainly.' She was rising and reaching for the old-fashioned bell rope, but Martineau said: 'Do you mind if we go and find him? I think Sergeant Errol knows his way around.'

'Not at all. He'll be in his pantry, I suppose.'

The two C.I.D. men departed and found the butler in his 'pantry', which was actually a very pleasant sitting room. He invited them in, made them comfortable, and offered liquor, which they refused.

Brandon looked at his watch, an old-fashioned gold dress watch. 'Tea then,' he said. 'It's near enough to four o'clock.' He pulled the tasselled bell rope, and a maid appeared. 'Tea for three, Smith,' he said.

While they waited for tea, Martineau acquainted him with the nature of the inquiry.

'And you wish to know if I heard or saw anything unusual last night?' the butler asked.

'Yes. Anything at all.'

'Well, I didn't, and I had my bedroom window open. I'm not at the back, you know. I'm at the side of the house, not very far from the front corner.'

'The corner nearest the gate?'

'Yes. It's a good listening post. Everything going

from front to back passes under my window. I knew all about Miss Caroline's frolics, long before they were brought to light by the police.'

'They're stopped now, I suppose?'

'I think so. I've heard nothing since.'

'Do all the staff know about that?'

Brandon smiled. 'Not through me, at any rate. But *I* know. I know most of what goes on in this house.'

'Have the maids got any, er, followers? You know, young fellows hanging around.'

Brandon looked thoughtful. 'They don't hang around the house, at any rate. But I did notice something only yesterday.'

The policemen looked expectant and interested. Brandon went on: 'It was in the village, near the entrance to the drive. Cook had sent Smith to the village shop for something or other. A little later I drove into town, to Oldham's the wine people. As I emerged from the drive I saw Smith in conversation with a young man. A tall, dark young man. I wouldn't say it was intimate conversation. They weren't standing close together. In fact they were about a yard apart. He was smiling, but her expression wasn't encouraging. I went on my way, and thought no more about it.'

'How was he dressed?'

Brandon looked disgusted. 'Dress? Do they dress nowadays? Tight trousers, jeans do they call them? Scuffed shoes. A blue, shapeless sort of jerkin thing. His hair needed cutting, but it wasn't as long as some I've seen.'

'Tall, you said. Was he well built?'

'Yes. Physically quite a fine fellow. Swarthy and rather deeply tanned. Nice teeth, I noticed.'

'And you made no more inquiries?'

'No. But I'll ask the girl when she brings the tea. Leave it to me. I'll get it out of her.'

So they gossiped until the tea came. Martineau perceived something which he had forgotten, that a butler in a household of this sort was a man of power. He ruled the rest of the staff, and only the cook and the housekeeper might not be in awe of him. His 'perks' would be considerable: whisky, cigars and so forth. No guest staying at the house would ever leave without giving him a tip, and a tip of less than five pounds would be an insult to him. It seemed that Mr. Brandon had a better job than most men.

The maid Smith arrived with tea, and a good-looking spread of biscuits and sandwiches. Martineau studied her. She would be no more than eighteen, of medium height, with a good, sturdy figure. She blushed when she sensed the D.C.I.'s appraisal. No doubt she would be sensitive about her sturdiness.

'Oh, Smith,' said Brandon casually, as she was about to depart. 'Just one moment. These gentlemen are from the police, as you might know. They are interested in a young man who has been hanging about this district. Who was that young man who spoke to you in the village yesterday?'

The pretty, artless young face became tense. The chin came up. Miss Smith was a young lady of spirit.

'I wasn't doing any wrong, Mr. Brandon.'

'I'm sure you weren't, Smith. Pretty girls do get spoken to. Who was the young man?'

'I don't know, sir. He was a foreigner of some sort.'

'Oh. What did he say?'

Colour came to the pretty face in full flood. She shook her head.

120

'Now, now, Smith. You must tell these gentlemen. It might be a clue.'

Smith was indignant. 'He was proper rude. He said I was a—a whopper.'

Two of the men retained their gravity with an effort, but Errol smiled. He said: 'The man wasn't insulting you, Miss Smith. He was speaking Spanish. The word "*guapa*" in Spanish is pronounced "wappa". It means "beautiful". He probably said: "*Que guapa*", which means: "What beauty". It was a compliment.'

The girl was embarrassed. 'Oh dear,' she said. 'I told him to go and get stuffed.'

Everybody laughed then, even the girl. Martineau asked: 'Did he seem to be hurt by the remark?'

'No. I walked away from him, but I looked back once, and he was still smiling and watching me.'

'Perhaps he didn't understand you,' said Errol. 'Anyway, if he *was* a Spaniard he would respect you for rebuffing him.'

They obtained a further description of the 'Spaniard' from the girl, and let her go. Other members of the staff were called in and questioned, but they had not seen the tall stranger.

The two policeman left the house and rounded off the inquiry in Kingsmead village. Only the village grocer remembered seeing the stranger. He had bought cigarettes at the shop, and he had spoken with a foreign accent. The shopkeeper's description of the man was similar to Brandon's, except that he described the jerkin as a 'donkey jacket'.

'I didn't know you spoke Spanish,' Martineau commented on the way back to Granchester.

'I don't,' said Errol. 'I was in Spain last year, on my Annual Leave. A place called San Feliu. I picked up a word or two. My wife told me about "wappa". It happened to her. A young Spaniard said it into her ear as he passed her in the street. Of course she wasn't satisfied till she'd found it in the dictionary.'

'Your wife must be a good-looking woman.'

'She's not bad,' said Errol modestly.

'Well, through her you've put us on the trail of something.'

'Aliens?'

'Yes. That fellow must be registered somewhere around here. And he sounds a bit like your dummy with the slumber thumb.'

14

The Granchester register of aliens produced no Spaniard who answered the description of the man seen in Kingsmead. Neither was there any luck in the neighbouring towns of Boyton and Sawford. But on the books at the County police divisional headquarters there was a certain Manuel Dominguez who answered the description. According to the record, he was employed by one Mildred Molyneux, at a house called Middle Pastures, near the village of Coverdale.

Errol and Cooper made the inquiry. When they read the address they looked hopefully at each other. Coverdale was eight or nine miles north-east of Granchester, and the distance was measured from the centre of Granchester. All the Dog Man burglaries had been committed in the suburbs which were on the Coverdale side of Granchester, so that coming and going on his raids a thief living in the village would have had no need to pass through the city. Also, Kingsmead on the east of the city could be reached by quiet byways from Coverdale.

Then the County Aliens Officer said something which made the City men stare. 'You'll have heard of Mrs. Molyneux,' he said. 'She's the dog woman. Labradors. She wins prizes all over the shop. Cruft's an' all.'

Errol and Cooper wasted no time in getting to Coverdale. They found Middle Pastures, a good-looking country house. Their arrival was greeted by a canine chorus. Mrs. Molyneux appeared. She was definitely a country-house sort of person; a tall strong woman in her middle fifties, with grey hair and a weathered face. She was dressed in tweed, and she wore brogues.

When the detectives had introduced themselves, her first words were: 'Did you close the gate properly?'

Errol replied that the gate was secure. It had not been the sort of gate to leave insecure. The gate, and the walls and fences which were the perimeter of the fields adjacent to the house, were heavily wired.

'You take precautions,' he said, with reference to the wire.

'I have to,' she replied. 'A stray dog amongst my bitches could cost me a lot of money. Then of course there are dog thieves.'

'Do you employ a man called Dominguez? Manuel Dominguez?'

She shook her head. 'I had to let Dominguez go.'

'Oh. Recently?'

'He finished at the week-end.'

'Unsatisfactory?'

'Yes,' she said. 'A good man with the dogs, but, er, unreliable.'

'Dishonest?'

Mrs. Molyneux's glance was level. 'Why are you seeking Dominguez?'

Errol met the glance. 'We want him, if he's the man we think he is. We're not sure until we see him.'

'I see. Well, Dominguez didn't steal anything from me. I employed him as a night man with the dogs. Part watchman, part kennelman. On two occasions I was disturbed in the night, and found that he had deserted his post. His explanations were not satisfactory. Of course he doesn't speak much English.'

'He's a Spaniard?'

'Yes. At least he says so. He certainly isn't English.'

'What time of the night was he missing?'

'From before one in the morning, for two or three hours. He was always back before daylight.'

'Have you got another watchman?'

'No, not yet. But a couple of my dogs are pugnacious. I lock up the bitches and let those two loose at night. They'll keep stray dogs away. Thieves too.'

Errol looked at the dogs he could see. Each animal had a big kennel and a long, fenced run. There were Labradors in the full range of colour from jet black to pale gold, and most of them looked friendly. Whether they would be friendly in the middle of the night was another matter.

'Beautiful creatures,' he said, and Mrs. Molyneux looked pleased.

She said: 'If ever your little boy wants a puppy you can bring him here. But of course I don't *give* them away.'

'Of course not. Could you give me a description of Dominguez?'

She obliged, and her description tallied with Brandon's.

'Have you any idea where he is now?'

'Not the slightest.'

'When he worked for you, did he live in the village?'

'No. He had a bed in the stable loft, and his breakfast in my kitchen. I don't know where he got the rest of his meals.'

'Do you have horses?'

'I have two. Incidentally, Dominguez is pretty good with horses.'

'He's even better with dogs, if he's the man we think he is. *If* he is that man, he can go into houses without being challenged by watchdogs.'

'Is that so?' Mrs. Molyneux looked interested. Then she was thoughtful. Her thoughts made her nostrils distend as if there was a bad smell around. She made a slight grimace of disgust.

'I wonder.' she said. 'Yesterday I found some very dirty overalls in the bottom of a bitch's kennel. The bitch was in season. Perhaps that is how Dominguez got by the watchdogs.'

'By wearing the overalls over his trousers, when he went to break-in somewhere? Yes, we had thought of that.'

'Nasty, isn't it?'

The detectives agreed that it was, though perhaps not nasty enough to worry a gypsy. They learned that Mrs. Molyneux had burned the overalls. They thanked her and left her then. They made some inquiries in Coverdale, but nobody there seemed to know anything about Manuel Dominguez.

'Taking a chance, wasn't she?' Cooper commented

with reference to Mrs. Molyneux, as they rode back to Granchester.

'Yes. A foreigner with nobody to vouch for him. The fact that he slept in the stable speaks for itself. He would work for low wages, but was given bed and breakfast. She wouldn't be able to get a local man on those terms.'

'He could afford to work for nothing. She must have a hundred dogs. If half of them are bitches, he would always be able to find one or two in season.'

'Yes. Anyway, it'll stop now.'

'I hope you're right. No more Dog Man jobs.'

'Unless he sneaks up to the kennels in the night. The dogs will know him.'

'We'll have to tip off the County about that.'

'Yes. I suppose they'll detain him when he goes in to register as an alien.'

'*When* he does. *If* he does. He just might make himself hard to find.'

'Where do we start to look?'

'We put out the word. We check all the places where he might try to get a job. Horses, dogs, a waiter, maybe. Waiter or barman. He's got all his chairs at home, has that hombre.'

'He'll probably move right out of this district.'

'Well, he hasn't showed signs of it yet, has he? Hanging around Kingsmead.'

'Going up to the Hall, too. That Dobermann would have torn him to pieces if he hadn't been wearing his *eau de chien*.'

'What's that?'

'It's French. You wouldn't understand, Sarge.'

'I would if you pronounced it right. I went to a Grammar School an' all, you know. Anyway, it's not

French we'll be wanting for this character.'
'You'll put it all on Martineau's lap?'
'But of course. I'm only a sergeant. He is the great
I Am on this job.'
'Well, he knows what he's looking for now.'
'Yes. And I'll bet you he finds it.'

15

Chief Inspector Martineau was not unduly disappointed to learn that Manuel Dominguez had left the
Molyneux kennels where he could have been so easily
picked up. Now, Dominguez was known. His description had been circulated throughout England, Scotland, Wales, and Northern Ireland. Interpol had been
informed, and they would pass on the information to
Dublin and Madrid. The police message stated that he
was 'wanted for interview in connection with the murder of Sir Richard Falcon'. Also, that he was suspected
of burglary and known to be violent.

Martineau thought about Dominguez. A Spanish
gypsy who spoke very little English; afraid to report
as an alien, and therefore unable to get a job. In any
case the Ministry of Labour had been informed. If
Dominguez called at any employment exchange he
would be detained there while the police were called.
He did not have a chance of remaining at liberty or
getting out of the country. No doubt he would have a
certain amount of stolen money in his possession,
but that would not last for ever. When the money was
done he might commit more burglaries, but probably
not at houses where dogs were kept. However, the

search for him had been given newspaper publicity. The national dailies had made quite a stir about it. More or less everybody in the country knew about Manuel Dominguez. Sooner or later he would be caught, and Martineau rather expected that it would be sooner.

Of course it crossed the D.C.I.'s mind that those other Spanish gypsies up on the edge of the moors might know something about Dominguez, but he did not immediately approach them. He waited until he could approach their friend Jesse Smith without their knowledge. This was in the morning hours when it was expected that the Spaniards would be sleeping late after their night-club activities. He informed the County police of his intention, and drove up to the little encampment with Devery. Jesse Smith was not hard to find. He was sitting on the steps of his caravan, enjoying a smoke in the morning sun.

'It's a grand morning,' Martineau greeted him.

'Beautiful,' Smith agreed. 'Especially for somebody who hasn't got a lot of work to do.'

'Like you,' said the detective with a smile.

'Like me,' was the stolid reply.

Martineau inclined his head towards the other caravan. 'Your friends not about yet?'

'They'll still be asleep, I expect.'

'Three of them, aren't there? Father, son and daughter.'

'That's right.'

'Were there ever more than three?'

'No, not living there. A young fellow used to come now and again, but I haven't seen him for two or three weeks.'

'What was he like?'

Smith gave a good description of Manuel Dominguez. Martineau asked: 'Did you ever hear his name?'

' "Manolo", they called him. I never heard his other name.'

The policeman did not know that 'Manolo' was the Spanish diminutive of 'Manuel', but he made a good guess. He asked: 'Does he live around here?'

Smith shrugged. 'I never asked. I believe he works at some kennels somewhere.'

Martineau remembered the first police visit to the caravans, when the lost white poodle had been found there. So it had not been an entirely false lead. There *had* been some connection with the Dog Man, after all.

He wondered if any of these people here had been criminally involved with Dominguez. Well, Smith had spoken quite freely about the man. It did not look as if *he* had any guilty involvement, at any rate. It did not look so. Smith's apparent willingness to talk might be false candour. He might know perfectly well that Dominguez no longer worked as a kennelman. He might be pretending to be helpful in order to divert suspicion from himself.

'And he hasn't been here for weeks?'

'I don't know. It's two or three weeks since I saw him.' Smith turned his head and spoke over his shoulder. 'Maria, have you seen Manolo lately?'

'Two or three Sundays since,' came his wife's reply.

'There you are,' said Smith. 'He usually comes on Sundays.'

'H'm. Do you ever read a newspaper?'

'Very seldom. They won't deliver up here.'

'Television?'

Smith shook his head. 'Radio,' he said. 'But the batteries are down and I keep forgetting to get new ones. Should I have heard summat in the news?'

Martineau did not answer. He looked at his watch, and then at the Segura caravan. 'I wonder if it's too early to wake Mr. Segura.'

'I generally hear 'em getting home about three, and they go straight to bed.'

The time was a little after ten: not much too early, at any rate. Then the problem was solved for him. The upper half of the Segura caravan door was thrown open. Conchita appeared. She seemed to be wearing a wrapper or dressing gown over night attire. When she saw the visitors she moved back out of sight.

'Thank you, Mr. Smith,' said Martineau. 'We'll hear what Mr. Segura has to say.'

He and Devery walked towards the other caravan. Salvador Segura appeared at the door. 'Good morning,' he said.

'Morning. Could we have a word with you?'

'Si—yes. *Momento.*' Salvador disappeared.

'*Momento,*' Martineau said to Devery. 'In a moment. Simple, isn't it?'

Devery grinned. 'Wait till he says something else.'

The door of the caravan was fully opened. Salvador appeared in shirt and trousers, and a strong one-day's growth of beard. He sat on the steps, and it could be seen that he had cigarettes and a lighter in his hands.

'*Cigarillo?*' he offered, and the detectives accepted cigarettes and a light. Salvador inhaled smoke contentedly, apparently a man without worries.

'Has Manolo been here lately?' Martineau asked.

Salvador was instantly serious. 'Manolo? He do— bad?'

Martineau shrugged. 'We don't know. No savvy.'

Salvador appeared to understand. He said: 'Manolo here *Domingo*.'

'*Domingo?*' Martineau was beaten. Devery grinned.

'*Domingo*,' said Salvador. 'Sunday.'

'Ah. Last Sunday?'

'Last?' Salvador did not understand the phrase. He projected three fingers. 'Sunday. *Tres dias passado*.'

Martineau grinned and looked triumphantly at Devery. 'You see?' he said. 'Sunday, three days past. Last Sunday in fact.'

'Last Sunday?' said Salvador anxiously, and when Martineau nodded he also nodded in satisfaction. He had learned another English phrase.

'What time?' the policeman asked, and was understood.

'Three o'clock,' said Salvador proudly. '*Tres horas*.'

'Thank you. What work does he do now?'

'Work? Manolo?' Salvador thought, and the word came to him. 'Dogs. Many dogs.'

'Where?'

Salvador waved vaguely in a northerly direction, and shrugged. '*Noche*,' he said. 'Work at night.'

Martineau shook his head. 'Not now.'

'Not now?' Salvador looked surprised. Then he thought of something. He said: 'Not with dogs. With horses.'

'No,' said Martineau. 'Not now. He's left there. Vamoosed.'

Salvador appeared to be bewildered, and vaguely distressed. Manolo had changed his job, and had not told him. Apparently the police were seeking him because he had not told them, either.

At that moment Jose appeared. Salvador gave him

the news in machine-gun Spanish. Jose shrugged, and gave an uninterested answer, and went away to the toilet.

'We won't learn anything here,' Martineau said to Devery. He said 'Good morning' to Salvador, and turned away. There was a chance that Manuel Dominguez might call again to see his friends. He decided to ask the County police to set a day-time watch on the caravans. And even that might be a waste of time. Dominguez seemed to be trusting nobody. He might have cut loose completely from the Segura family.

Martineau had done all that he could about Manuel Dominguez, but he did not cease to think about him. The man's two appearances at Kingsmead were a puzzling development. The midnight appearance might have been a reconnaissance with burglary in mind, but what on earth had he been doing in the village in the middle of the day? Not for the purpose of scraping acquaintance with one of the maids from the Hall, Martineau felt sure. That meeting with Miss Smith in the village had been a chance in a thousand, and probably Dominguez had not known who she was. Words had been exchanged merely as a result of the Spaniard's amorous impulses. So, what *had* he been doing in Kingsmead?

Devery was passing the back door of the Tahiti Club that afternoon, and he saw that the door was open. A wine-and-spirit merchant's van was near the door. Devery entered, and went along to the manager's office, where the wine merchant's driver was watching the manager sign the delivery note. The driver picked up the note and departed. Devery stood in the open doorway of the office.

'Hello,' said the manager. 'You can't come in here without a warrant.'

'In that case,' said Devery, 'I'll go and get one.'

The manager's name was Sinclair, and he was a new man. But he already knew most of the A Division C.I.D. He was youngish, rotund and shrewd, and he *seemed* to enjoy the company of policemen. Now, he laughed to show that his curt remark had been a joke, just to be sure that Devery had not taken him seriously.

'Come on in,' he said. 'What'll you have to drink?'

'Nothing at the moment, thank you,' the sergeant replied. 'I happened to see the door open and I wondered how you were getting on with your Spaniards.'

'Oh, fine.' Sinclair replied without hesitation. 'They look like being here for the duration. They're good, you know. And the lads like to look at the *señorita*.'

'Well, she's worth it.'

'She sure is. A real Spanish beauty. I hope she's doing all right for herself with young Falcon.'

'Falcon? You mean Peter Falcon?'

'*Sir* Peter to you. Yes, it's on. It's no secret. He's here every night. She goes and sits at his table. He drives her home.'

'The old man lets him do that?'

'Sure. Whatever happens, she can't go wrong with somebody as rich as him, can she? I remember when they met. She threw her scarf at Falcon's feet and he picked it up and chased her behind the curtain. I figured then that the old man was thinking about going for his knife, and his son was just waiting for the word from him. I got to 'em in time, and told 'em who Falcon actually was. So that was all right. Their Spanish pride wasn't proof against a title and a million quid.'

Devery was thoughtful. 'How about when young Falcon wants to break?'

'Easy, I should think. A nice little settlement. A few thousand quid'll do wonders. Then the whole family'll be off back to the Spanish sunshine, to open their own club.'

'Boy,' said Devery, apparently dismissing the matter. 'It must be great to have your old man leave you a fortune. I call that being born lucky.'

'Yes. The lad seems to have everything you could wish for. What made you interested in the Segura family?'

'Only because of that other Spaniard we're looking for. You know, strangers in a foreign country. They stick together.'

'Do you want me to ask them if they know him?'

'No. Don't mention him. Are they still doing all right here?'

'You asked me that once.'

'So I did. Time I was on my way. Cheerio, then.'

'Cheerio,' the manager said.

Devery went to tell Martineau about the affair between Peter Falcon and Conchita Segura.

16

Conchita Segura told Sir Peter Falcon about Manuel Dominguez. 'He wish to marry me,' she said, 'and my father say no. He is strong, and he has a *cuchillo*.'

'Would he use it?' Peter asked, not greatly perturbed.

'Yes. When he is boy in Spain he kill a man.'

'Oh. That makes the matter more serious. Does he know about us?'

Conchita shrugged. 'Many peoples must know. Take care.'

Peter took care in his own way. He inspected the complete and almost unused tool kit of the Rolls and selected a big tyre lever. This he placed ready for use in the open dashboard cupboard of the car. After that he decided that he was ready for any Spaniard with a knife, and gave no more thought to the matter.

But in the small hours of Saturday morning, six days after Manolo's first sight of Peter and Conchita together, Peter was abruptly reminded of the danger of a Spaniard with a knife. The danger was made manifest at two-twenty-five, in Kingsmead village. P.C. Baines on his motor-cycle had been and gone, and he had observed nothing to be suspicious about. The village was sound asleep, and there was no traffic passing through. It was the quietest part of the night.

The night was clear and dark, and as Peter turned the nose of the Rolls into the entrance to the Falcon estate he was using headlights. Twenty-five yards inside the gateway, a man was standing in the middle of the drive, in an attitude which suggested that he had no intention of moving. Well, Peter had been warned. His car had not yet gathered speed after the turn, and he was able to stop in a yard or two. The stranger moved towards the car at once.

Peter did not wait in the car. He stepped out, picked up the tyre lever, and moved to the front of the car. He stood with the headlights behind him, having no intention of fighting in the dark. He had no feeling of fear, but was strongly curious about what was likely to happen.

Four yards away from Peter, the stranger stopped. His eyes were fixed on the bright new tyre lever. Peter was holding it across his body, with one end of it in each hand, so that he could use it with either hand at need. The light from the lamps was not shining directly upon it, and to the other man it looked like a machete, a weapon far more dangerous than a knife.

The two young men faced each other in silence, then Peter said: '*Buenos noches, señor. Usted Manolo Dominguez?*'

Manolo replied that he was, and then there was a brief conversation in rough Andaluz and very bad Castilian, to the effect that Conchita Segura was the sweetheart of Manolo, with a contradiction that Conchita was *not* for Manolo. While this little argument took place, Manolo edged round to Peter's left, so that he did not have headlights shining in his eyes. Peter turned to face him.

Manolo's knife appeared. He moved in quickly with the knife held low. The tyre iron flicked out at him. He ducked, but the edge of the iron caught him on the side of the forehead. The blow stopped him, and his deadly upward thrust with the knife was not completed.

The blow on the head may have dazed him, because when Peter followed up he did not get up his guard in time, and he was hit on the head again. Manolo fell sideways against the radiator of the car. As he heaved himself upright Peter used the flat of the tyre lever to hit him with great force on the side of the jaw. Manolo collapsed.

Peter took Manolo's knife, and threw it into the cricket field. He 'frisked' him for other weapons and found none.

Manolo's face was a mask of blood from his cut forehead. Peter bandaged him with the large silk handkerchief from his breast pocket. Then he took him under the arms and dragged him round to the passenger side of the car. He opened the door and managed to get the apparently unconscious man on to the nearside front seat, with his legs in the road. He was stooping to lift the legs and feet into the car when one knee came up hard under his jaw. He reeled backwards badly shaken, but kept on his feet. He turned away to get the tyre lever, which was lying in the road in front of the car. He did not intend to use it again now that Manolo was disarmed, but it would be a threat to keep him quiet.

When he turned again with the lever in his hand, he saw that his late antagonist had managed to move into the car's driving seat. When he ran to pull open the door he realised that Manolo had known how to lock it from inside. As he moved around trying the other doors he heard the brief chirp of the starter.

The car moved forward, then turned and broke through the low fence of the cricket field. It went out into the field and began to circle back towards the drive. Peter ran for his life towards the village.

As he ran through the estate gateway on his way to the telephone box, he realised that Manolo was quite capable of driving the big car straight at the box and crushing him inside. He also realised that the solid stone of the gateway was his best safeguard. He remained there, and was just round the corner when the car came through.

He was seen. Manolo turned the car into the road, and reversed to come at him from that side. He ran through the gateway again and stood round the corner at the other side. Manolo came through again, and began to circle in the field. So Peter repeated the manœuvre.

Manolo drove through the gateway once more, and perhaps he realised that Peter was out of his reach. He drove away towards Granchester.

Peter emerged and watched until the glow of headlights could no longer be seen. He wondered, would Manolo return in the hope of catching him in the telephone kiosk? 'Home, boy, home,' he decided, and began to run up the drive.

The car did not return. Peter was met at the gate by the dog Rajah, who was soberly pleased to see him. In the house he picked up the telephone and dialled 9-9-9. He gave his number and asked for the police.

The police came on the line in a second or two. Peter gave his name and reported the theft of the Rolls, giving the number, colour and model.

'Where last seen, sir?' the police operator wanted to know.

'Ten or fifteen minutes ago, going from Kingsmead towards town. The driver has a bandaged head and a lot of blood on his face. He said his name was Manuel Dominguez.'

'Manuel Dominguez? You're sure of that?'

'I asked him if his name was Manolo Dominguez, and he said Yes in Spanish. Manolo is short for Manuel.'

'I see. Thank you, sir. We'll get your statement later. There seem to be certain, er, circumstances about this. The blood, and you knowing his name and that. Can I ring you back in a few minutes?'

'Yes. I'll wait.'

The word about the Rolls and its driver was put out by radio, and by telephone to neighbouring police forces. Unfortunately, the message to the neighbours did not stress the information about the driver's head injuries, and it was not assumed that he would go to a hospital. The Rolls was found in daylight at half-past four in the forecourt of Boyton General Hospital, eight miles from Granchester. Inquiries revealed that a young man had had six stitches put in his head, and had been allowed to depart.

'Martineau will go up in the air,' predicted the A Division night-duty inspector. 'He'll go stone doo-lalley. Dominguez could have been picked up dead easy at the hospital while he was having his head stitched.'

'Good job it happened in Boyton,' the station sergeant said. 'We're in the clear. I wonder if Dominguez is hanging out in Boyton.'

Actually, at that moment Manolo was nursing his aching head in the stable loft at Middle Pastures. He had left a window unfastened when he ceased to be employed by Mrs. Molyneux. So long as he was not seen, he could come and go at his leisure. The dogs knew him and they made no trouble. He was comfortable in the loft, and there was no landlady and no fellow lodgers to get curious about him. Also, he was saving bed money, an important matter to him. Eventually someone would find him, he supposed. That was something which he would worry about when the time came. The thing which did worry him at that time was the fact that he had lost his knife. He realised that he would have to get another one somewhere if he was going to make an end of his rival for the affections of Conchita Segura.

He thought about that until he fell asleep, and it was the first thing to come into his mind when he awoke. His head still ached, but less fiercely than before, so he assumed that it would eventually cure itself. He rubbed grime from the window of the loft, and saw that the weather had broken. It was raining steadily. That was good fortune for him, he thought. Part of his bedding was an old duffle coat with a hood. He tried it and found that it was almost big enough for him. So he was equipped against the rain, and the hood would cover his bandage to some extent.

Wearing his duffle coat he sneaked out of the stables, and got away from Middle Pastures without being seen. At the pastrycook's shop in Coverdale he bought two meat pies, and ate them as he walked along. He noticed that the public houses were open, and he called for a pint of beer, but only stayed in the inn long enough to drink the beer. Then he set out to walk by byways familiar to him, to Granchester to buy a knife. The rain soon soaked through his shoddy shoes, but that did not trouble him. He could buy new shoes in Granchester too.

Chief Inspector Martineau sought out Sir Peter Falcon at Kingsmead Hall, to hear for himself the story of the nocturnal encounter.

'You were lucky,' he said when he had listened. 'Dominguez might have thrown that knife.'

Peter did not think so. 'No,' he said. 'I got the feeling that it was a sort of duel at first. He admitted his identity, and told me what we were fighting about. It was only after I'd tried to put him in the car that it ceased to be a fair fight. With the car he was really murderous, and I *was* lucky then, to have some cover.

I was going to take him to a hospital, but he may have thought I was taking him to a police station.'

'Either way you would have informed the police, I suppose.'

'I suppose so,' Peter admitted. 'I wonder if he'll have another go at me.'

'Possibly. You'll have to be alert. Do you want police protection?'

'No. My sister won't have it either. I'm afraid of her getting a bad fright.'

'You'll have to enlist the Seven Foot Four as a guard of honour.'

Peter looked disgusted. 'That gang! Long-haired nitwits! I don't know why Carol wants to fool around with such people.'

Martineau thought how the duel might easily have wrapped up the whole case. He sighed with savage regret. 'Our worries would have been over if certain police officers hadn't been walking about with their brains asleep. It's maddening.'

'Yes. I'm sorry about that.'

'No blame to you. But if you meet Dominguez again, don't let him get the better of you. Did anything occur to you about him, when you fought him?'

'No, but it has since. Could he be the man who killed my father?'

'We think so. And quite probably he doesn't know he's suspected of that. He's confident, you know. He's hard to catch and he knows it. But I'm damned if I know why we can't manage to find him. An alien who doesn't speak the language! He should stand out like Nelson on his column. Now he's got a bandaged head with six stitches, and we still can't get a smell of him.'

'You'll find him one of these days, sir.'

'The sooner the better. And you watch out. You know what his intentions are now.'

'He might have had enough of me.'

'He's got a score to settle. You be alert.'

And with that Martineau departed. On his way down the drive he stopped his car near the scene of the fight. He searched around in the cricket field and saw Manolo's knife shining in the sun. On his way to the laboratory with the knife he made the resolve to have two C.I.D. men at Kingsmead Hall every night from ten o'clock onwards.

At the laboratory the forensic scientists failed to find even the slightest trace of blood either on the blade or hilt of the knife, though it was the same size as the knife which had killed Sir Richard Falcon. Martineau was disappointed. It began to look as if evidence of murder against Dominguez was going to be very thin.

17

The story of Peter's fight and the subsequent taking of his car did not reach the ears of the Press. Nor had he intended to tell his mother or his sister about it. But the broken fence of the cricket field and a few scratches on the Rolls-Royce led to a domestic inquiry. Peter was a poor liar, and eventually both Lady Falcon and Caroline found out all about it.

The day after this inquiry, friend-of-the-family Robbie Weston called at Kingsmead Hall. He discerned that Lady Falcon was deeply troubled about something, and very soon he knew the story as well. He went in search of Peter and found him in Sir

Richard's study, which was now more or less his own.

He was invited to sit, and was offered a drink, which he accepted. But he wasted no time.

'I hear you've been in the wars,' he said.

'A bit of a scuffle, Uncle Robbie.'

'Over that Spanish girl you've been running around with?'

'Yes,' said Peter, but he frowned.

'None of my business, you think?'

'Well . . . You're not my father, or my guardian.'

'I'm your godfather, Peter. With your father gone, I have a duty, and a right.'

Peter was silent.

'How old are you, twenty-three?'

Peter nodded.

'Half the town knows about you and the girl. Do you intend to marry her?'

'I wouldn't mind. But it wouldn't do. She wouldn't fit in here.'

'Does she know that?'

'Yes. We've talked about it, and she's sensible. She knows it won't last forever.'

'And what does that get her?'

'Money, I suppose.'

Weston raised his eyebrows.

'Don't get me wrong,' said Peter. 'I'm not *buying* the girl's affections. When I speak of money, I mean an honourable settlement.'

'Does she know that?'

'In a way. I've told her she'll never be sorry she met me.'

Weston was relieved to learn of an arrangement which he regarded as sensible. But he said: 'Suppose you put her in the family way?'

'I'm sufficiently well-informed to prevent any such happening. But if it does happen, I'll see that she isn't ruined.'

Weston realised that there was no more to be said, but there was another matter on his mind. He pursued: 'I'm *not* Caroline's godfather, but I feel a responsibility for her. And so should you.'

'Well, I do, but I can't do much about it. She has her own money now. Or will have very soon. She doesn't take one damn bit of notice of what I say.'

'That drug case was very unsavoury, and the papers had her walking with the fellow. Whatsisname, Deluce.'

'Yes. I told her it was a bad show. She just looked haughty and walked away from me. She wants her backside leathering, but I'm afraid she's just a bit too grown up for it.'

'Could we do anything with the fellow?'

Peter brightened. 'You mean give him a damned good hiding? Make him keep away from my sister?'

'Steady, Peter. That might make things worse. She might run off with him. You could have a chat with him, and see how it goes.'

Peter thought about that. 'Yes, I could have a word with him. Thanks, Uncle Robbie. I understand how you feel you want to help.'

Peter said to Caroline: 'I think I ought to meet this fellow of yours.'

Said Caroline: 'You're not going to meet him if you're going to act like an insufferable snob.'

'Ho. Ho. You're like a mother hen. I know how to talk to a man of my own age.'

'Well, if you start a fight you might get a shock.'

Peter affected to be surprised and hurt. 'Who said

anything about starting a fight? We're not living in the Stone Age.'

'I know you. Attend to your own affairs and leave mine alone. *You've* got nothing to preach about.'

'Well, I'm not a drug addict, at any rate.'

This so enraged Caroline that she started a fight herself. Her hand came round to deliver a slap that would have hurt, but Peter ducked. When she attacked again he caught her wrists. She tried to kick him, but could not reach his shins. Tears of mortification started in her eyes. He released her and she went away in a fury.

After that Peter let the matter stew for a few days, then he appeared at Leo Deluce's flat at eleven o'clock on a Sunday morning.

Johnny Revill let him into the flat. Revill was obviously bathed but not yet shaven. He was wearing a pink shirt and blue trousers with a red stripe.

'I'm Peter Falcon,' the visitor began. 'Are you Leo Deluce?'

'No. My name is Revill. Leo is having a shower. He'll be out in a minute. Sit you down, I'm just making some coffee.'

Peter sat, and lit a cigarette. Very soon Revill appeared with the coffee, and then Deluce came. He too was unshaven, in a white T-shirt and jeans. Peter rose to meet him.

'I'm Peter Falcon,' he said.

'Yes, I know. I'm Leo Deluce. Glad to meet you, but are we friends or enemies?'

'I don't know yet,' said Peter, but he offered his hand.

Deluce took the hand. The handshake was a brief trial of strength, and nobody was the winner. Deluce's gaze was level and unafraid.

Johnny Revill was an expressionless witness to the meeting. They all sat down, and Peter said to Deluce: 'I'd like to talk to you alone.'

Deluce shook his head. 'I have no secrets from Johnny. He'll stay. If you're thinking of a punch-up there's the backyard, but I don't want this flat breaking up. Some of these guitars are valuable. That one there is worth as much as that vintage Bentley of yours.'

He talks big, Peter thought. He did not believe that any guitar in the world was worth as much as his Bentley. But he realised that the decision to have Revill present showed common sense. Obviously, Deluce was a cool customer. His straightforward handling of the situation, and his obvious physical fitness, drew a reluctant approval from Peter.

'You don't look like a fellow who takes drugs,' he said.

'Don't I?'

'That's what I'm here about. I've got a sister, you know. I don't want her to get the drug habit.'

'Naturally you don't. But if she wants to take drugs, *I* can't stop her.'

'But you could start her? That's what is on my mind.'

'You need have no fear. She's never had any pot from me, and never will have. I don't have any. I can't afford to have any. If somebody gives me a reefer at a party, I might smoke it. But I don't have the habit, and never did have.'

'What about LSD, and that?'

'Not on your life. I don't want to go crackers.'

'Does Carol smoke reefers?'

'No. She has had one or two. But now she agrees

with me that it isn't worth while. It's old hat, anyway.'

'It's a mug's game.'

'Agreed.'

Whereupon Peter found himself with nothing to say. He tasted his coffee and found that it was good. He lit another cigarette. Then he said: 'But you *did* have some reefers when the police picked you up.'

'That's true.'

'Where did you get them?'

'Do you want me to put you in touch with a pusher?'

'You know damned well I don't. It's funny when you said you'd never had the habit. How many did you have?'

'When the coppers got me? Three. Three cigarettes.'

'Well, then.'

'You'd be surprised if you knew who they belonged to.'

'Were they Carol's?'

Deluce looked at him for some time, and then said: 'As I told you, Caroline doesn't smoke reefers.'

'But she did?'

'If she did, that's her own affair. She doesn't now, unless she's deceiving me. I suggest we talk about something else.'

'What else is there to talk about? I'm not interested in pop music.'

Revill said: 'I've seen you with the Spanish dancer from the Tahiti Club.'

Peter remembered just in time not to be haughty. He said: 'Yes. She's a friend of mine.'

'She's a beauty. And a lovely singer.'

'She's not bad,' said Peter modestly.

'That's the understatement of the year. I wonder if there are any more like that in Spain.'

'I wouldn't be surprised.' Peter looked at his watch. 'I'd better be going.'

'Have another cup of coffee.'

'No, thanks.' Peter stood up. The other two also left their chairs.

Deluce was cool, sardonic. 'Have you found out what you wanted to know?'

'Some of it. I haven't broken any squares, have I?'

They all grinned. Deluce said: 'You didn't get the chance, did you? You were talked out of it, but I didn't tell you any lies.'

They shook hands, and Peter left the flat. When he had gone, Deluce said: 'He seems all right, considering he had it all laid in his lap when he was born.'

As he walked to his car, Peter thought: I could get on with that character if he'd get his hair cut.

18

The weather changed again, to prove to the satisfaction of the English that during the infrequent periods when their weather *is* good, it is the best in the world. In the daytime mild sunshine blessed the countryside, and the nights were still and balmy. It was perfect courting weather, and it is to be feared that many babies were conceived in the hedgerows of that maytime. Caroline Falcon was happy with her Leo, Peter Falcon made the most of his time with Conchita, and Robbie Weston's visits to Kingsmead Hall were so frequent that it became obvious that he wished to be more than a friend of the family.

For some people there were certain flaws in these

ideal situations. To Weston's annoyance, Lord Geever also became a regular visitor to Kingsmead. On the pretext of visiting Peter, Larry Geever also visited Kingsmead a number of times, and showed a desire for Caroline's company. Leo Deluce learned about this, and it made him savagely uneasy. Conchita was nervous about Manuel Dominguez, and this was sometimes tedious for Peter, who was not nervous at all. The police appreciated the marvellous weather as much as anyone, but they failed to find the Dog Man, and the Falcon murder remained uncleared, and the temporarily perfect climate was turning out to be a great encouragement to lawbreakers of all kinds. The police were busy.

Manuel Dominguez made the best of a lonely and furtive existence without once losing sight of his objective, Peter Falcon. It was a point of honour that Peter should die, and in moments of melancholy Manolo sometimes thought that Conchita should die also. Indeed, Manolo was feeling disillusioned about the entire Segura family, and occasionally in daydreams he imagined an action in which both Salvador and Jose were slain. The epithet for Manolo's mood was 'bloody-minded', though apart from his vendetta with Peter Falcon—a matter of honour—he was not a cold-blooded murderer. He killed as a bull might kill, in rage or fear, but not in the pursuance of a plan.

But for Peter he made plans. This time, there was to be no mistake. By observation he had learned a lot about the Falcon family, and such was his desire for a consummate revenge that he even considered warring on its womenfolk. Peter's mother was a handsome woman, quite attractive to twenty-five-year-old Manolo. And the daughter, Peter's sister, was a pretty pullet. The assault and rape of either of those women would be calculated to drive young Falcon mad. Manolo often thought about that, without really intending that anything of the sort should happen.

The fine, warm weather was ideal for Manolo. For sleeping purposes he still used Mrs. Molyneux's stable loft occasionally, but he was no longer dependent on it. There was one very dense and secluded corner of Kingsmead Wood where he felt safe. Careful reconnaissance convinced him that nobody had been in that spot for a long time. Apparently neither the village boys nor the village lovers went there. In Granchester he bought a small green tent. He erected it in the wood and spent some time arranging camouflage and concealment. After that he felt sure that in an emergency he would have shelter and a safe hiding place.

The two C.I.D. men who spent the hours of darkness on watch at Kingsmead Hall usually perched themselves in the big beech tree near the gates where Errol and Cooper had once sought concealment. The Falcon family were informed of their presence, but otherwise might never have discovered them. Certainly Manolo, crafty gypsy though he was, did not spot them until they had occasion to show themselves, and that was one time when the police were there when they were wanted.

If they had not been there, Caroline Falcon would almost certainly have come to harm one summer midnight when she returned from Granchester. That night Manolo was on the prowl, and he had been thinking lustfully about both Caroline and her mother. He was in a dangerous mood, and either woman would have suited his purposes.

From the shelter of a hedge not far from the beech

tree, Manolo saw the lights of Caroline's small open car as it came from the direction of the village. On an impulse he left his concealment and ran towards the gate. When Caroline stopped her car at the gate he was only a few strides away. He was beside her before she could get out to open the gate, where the dog Rajah was waiting. He showed her his knife and said: 'No noise.' It was a wasted threat because Rajah was already jumping at the gate and roaring at him.

Because of the knife at her throat Caroline did not scream or struggle as Manolo pulled her out of the car. She kept her feet but he tripped her and knocked her down. She was getting up when he kicked her in the face, and she collapsed. Then Manolo had time to look around, and he saw two men running from the direction of the beech tree. He reacted like lightning. The car's engine was still running. He slipped into the driver's seat and put the car into gear, and it began to move when the nearest of the two men was still fifteen yards away. He drove in a wide circle on the grass and back to the driveway, and away towards the village. The two panting C.I.D. men swore bitterly. It was common knowledge in the force that the man who caught Manuel Dominguez would be in line for promotion, and who else could that fellow have been?

As it happened, Peter Falcon came home earlier than usual that night. He was driving his open Bentley, and he slowed to go through the archway on to his own land when Manolo emerged driving Caroline's car. Peter recognised the car, and had a good enough view of its driver to guess at his identity. Manolo turned away from Granchester, towards Kingsmead Wood. Peter was able to follow without having to turn his car.

Either Manolo drove very well, or he was reckless and lucky. On winding secondary roads Peter was not able to overtake with his big old Bentley. It soon became evident that Manolo was circling back to the city, and Peter felt sure of catching him on a good road. But Manolo had no intention of going into Granchester. He circled round to Westholme, and drove past the police station there, and down the hill where he had ridden P.C. Baines's motor-cycle. He stopped at the bridge there and abandoned the car. As he had done once before, he leaped down the steps and fled along the riverside path.

Peter did the same, and found that Manolo was a slightly better runner than himself. The two men ran for nearly a mile, past pretty little suburban houses. When the houses ceased, Manolo vaulted a gate into a field and ran across the field and over another gate into a wood. Peter stopped at the gate to the wood. Anxious though he was to come to grips with Señor Dominguez, he did not wish to meet him in a wood at midnight. On his way back to Westholme, he wondered why Manolo had not stopped to fight him on the towpath, or in the field. Making his way through the wood, Manolo was wondering the same thing. Of course, he realised, it was the narrow escape from those two men at Kingsmead which had upset him. He now knew that he would have to be more careful. The Falcon family was getting police protection.

Chief Inspector Martineau heard about the affair when he arrived at his office at nine o'clock the following morning. Frowning he studied the account of police action. One car stolen, and recovered undamaged. A wood near Westholme surrounded (probably an hour after the fugitive had departed) and searched at daylight. First aid rendered to Miss Caroline Falcon. Miss Falcon had escaped serious injury. The kick in the face had perhaps been rather perfunctory. Her jaw and one ear were bruised and swollen, but there was no fracture. She was now in bed, suffering from shock. Sir Peter Falcon had chased her assailant, but had failed to overtake him. Sir Peter was reasonably certain that he had been chasing Manuel Dominguez. That was all.

Martineau congratulated himself on his foresight in putting two men on guard at Kingsmead Hall. At least they had saved Caroline from serious harm. Rape? Probably. A sort of revenge. A thwarted gypsy's idea of rough justice, maybe. But his men had let the gypsy escape them again. The man's promptitude in evasive action was phenomenal. It was perhaps not surprising that in the Spanish countryside the police were armed with rifles. They caught men like Dominguez with bullets.

Martineau saw no reason why he should go to Kingsmead, but Chief Superintendent Clay could see one very adequate reason.

'They're big people,' he said. 'And they tell me Lord Geever's getting middling friendly there. You have a run out there and see how they're taking it.'

So Martineau drove to Kingsmead Hall, and asked to see Lady Falcon. He saw her, and was surprised to see her taking a drink at ten o'clock in the morning.

'It's brandy,' she said. 'I go into a dither whenever I think of what might have happened to Caroline.'

'It's a good thing two of our men were there,' said Martineau, taking the opportunity to remind her of that.

'It is indeed. I can't thank them enough. But whatever are we going to do about this—this maniac?'

'Police protection is the answer, as it has already proved to be.'

'A policeman in the house? I don't think I shall feel safe in my own room now.'

'Well, we don't have an unlimited number of men to spare for bodyguard duty, but I'll see what can be done. Where is the dog?'

'Chained to his kennel at the kitchen door.'

'You should have him in the house, and have all outer doors locked.'

Lady Falcon sighed. 'Yes, I suppose so. Such lovely weather, too.'

'How is Miss Caroline?'

'Oh, she'll be all right. She's been having brandy, too. Now she's sitting up in bed, having some breakfast.'

'And Sir Peter?'

'I believe he's just getting up. He was very late to bed. He went with the police to surround that wood.'

'He very nearly caught the man, I believe.'

'I'm glad he didn't. Caroline told me about that awful knife the man had. I think Peter should carry a pistol.'

'I don't think the Chief Constable would allow that. A police bodyguard would be better.'

'I don't think he'll have that.' Again Lady Falcon sighed. 'It's the Spanish girl. He won't have a policeman around when he's with her.'

Martineau was thoughtful. He said: 'We have one dog here, but I keep thinking that police dogs would be useful. They have their own handlers, but one of them could be sort of seconded to Sir Peter. He would

soon make friends with it. It would go around with
him.'

'I think that's a wonderful idea. But would he bring
it home with him?'

'At night, yes. But we could have the handler take
it from him at the gate.'

'Yes, of course. We couldn't do with Rajah killing
a police dog.'

Martineau thought of the police Alsatians. One of
them might kill Rajah. Or probably the two dogs
would kill each other.

'No, we couldn't have that,' he said. 'But I'll see
what I can arrange. In the meantime I want you to
make sure that neither yourself nor Miss Caroline goes
out alone.'

Lady Falcon shuddered. 'Neither of us will,
Inspector.'

19

Chief Inspector Martineau had sent an inquiry about
the Chinaman known as 'Bob Eye' to every big police
force in the country. The most promising reply had
come from the Drugs Branch of the Metropolitan
Police at New Scotland Yard. It had come via Chief
Superintendent Coulson of the Yard. He had worked
with Martineau. Once Martineau had been a great
help to him, and once he had been a great help to Martineau, and the two men were friends. The message
was the description of a man who had been questioned and searched a number of times by detective
officers on suspicion of carrying illicit drugs, but he

still had no criminal record. The description had been taken from the cross-index of suspects with physical peculiarities, and he was the only Chinaman on the index with a marked eye peculiarity. The description was somewhat informal because the index was only semi-official. Thus:

'Chu Sen Su, born Whitechapel, London, 1922, of Chinese parents. Medium height and build, black hair, sallow complexion, Mongoloid eyes and features. Left eye is a blank, pale, bloodshot grey without pupil, and apparently sightless. Chu sometimes wears dark glasses and sometimes a black eye patch, and sometimes no eye cover at all. He usually wears a dark suit and is respectably dressed. No fixed abode, never been known to work for a living, and seems to like blondes. Speaks Cockney without the Chinese lisp. Seems able to converse with Lascars and Chinese seamen in their own language. Very glib talker. Never been known to be violent.'

It seemed, then, that Chu Sen Su spent most of his time in London. He would only visit Granchester when he had surplus drugs for sale, and perhaps occasionally to meet a crew member from a ship in Sawford Docks. No doubt he dealt in opium and heroin as well as cannabis resin. 'I'll bet he's our Bob Eye,' said Martineau.

He made no more inquiries about the man, for fear of alerting his associates. He spoke to the inspector of policewomen, and arranged for London trains, London planes, and buses from London to be met at their termini. The policewomen—in plain clothes—were not likely to miss seeing a Chinaman with dark glasses, an eye patch, or a blind eye. They were instructed to avoid contact with the man, and to remain unobserved if possible. Their duty would be to report the man's presence, and to follow him surreptitiously. When the man had been located, they would be assisted by male detectives with a car.

That was all there was to be done, and it was done efficiently during the June days and nights while all the things happened which led to the necessity for the Falcon family to be guarded. Leo Deluce had been fined and told to go and sin no more. Peter Falcon had been attacked, and so had Caroline. Peter and Leo had met, and each had conceived a reluctant respect for the other. Martineau still hunted the Dog Man, and P.C. Baines still nursed his hopeful feeling that there would be yet another happening at Kingsmead Hall.

Chu Sen Su alighted from the London train just before noon at Granchester's South Midland Station, on the last Monday in June. He was spotted simultaneously by Policewomen Rosamund Valentine and Susan Brown, from different parts of the arrival platform. They rushed together, agog. Then Valentine, the senior, told Brown to calm down a bit, and they followed Chu more carefully.

Because of the possibility that if Chu arrived by train he might take a taxi at the station, a C.I.D. car was waiting there. But outside the station Chu did not take a taxi. His only luggage was a rather tightly packed briefcase, and he walked out of the station and down the long station approach. There were not many pedestrians on that bare stretch of roadway, and Valentine thought that she and Brown would be very noticeable if they followed Chu on foot. Detective Constable Norton, in the police car, had seen them and was watching them. Valentine turned and beckoned. He came along and stopped the car beside them.

157

'That Chinese with dark glasses,' she said, pointing. 'We'd better not walk after him. We'll let him get to the bottom of the approach and then ride down.'

They watched until the Chinaman turned the corner at the foot of the slope. They followed, expecting to see him not very far away when they reached the corner themselves. But at the corner he was not in sight.

'Well, my goodness!' exclaimed Valentine in dismay. 'Where can he be?'

'In one of those shops, maybe,' said Norton. 'Or in that pub. Maybe he wanted a drink, and that's why he didn't take a cab. I'll go in the pub and look. You watch the shops.'

The public house was a small one, well-maintained as 'tied' houses usually are. It was called the Tudor Rose and—correctly in Norton's opinion—the rose was a red one as the inn sign showed. A white rose would, he thought, have been named Plantagenet. Inside the inn, he found that there was just a saloon bar and a public bar, with the serving bar between them.

It did not occur to Norton to go into the public bar because he knew that he would look out of place there. He suspected that he looked like what he was, the product of a good family and a good school. That was why he would tell his colleagues with a grin—he did not look like a policeman. He went into the saloon bar, and facing him in the public bar was a Chinaman. The man was cleaning his dark glasses with a paper tissue. His left eye was blank and sightless. He appeared not to look at Norton. Norton tried not to look at him after the first glance.

There seemed to be no other customers in the place,

and the man serving in the bar was almost certainly the licensee. He looked the right sort of person for a place of that size and type, a working man whose customers would be working men. Norton felt sure that this man had been talking to the Chinaman when he entered the place, but after Norton had been civilly greeted and served with a half-pint of bitter, there was no conversation at all. Norton took a newspaper from his pocket and pretended to read it. The landlord also picked up a newspaper. The Chinaman simply stood at the bar, expressionless behind his dark glasses.

Norton finished his drink and called at the toilet on his way out. This was on a short passage leading to the back door. When he came out of the toilet he heard a low murmur of talk in the bar. He went out of the place by the back door, which was actually at the side of the premises. It opened on to a wide passage which led to a small backyard. The passage was the only way out of the yard. So it seemed that anyone who quitted the inn, back door or front, would have to appear on the street where the C.I.D. car waited. One man could watch the place easily enough, and only one car would be needed.

But when he reached the street he saw that help had already arrived. P.W. Valentine had been using the car radio, seemingly, and she had moved the car. She was standing at the nearest corner, looking into a shop window, and no doubt the car would be round the corner. At the other end of the short row of shops, Detective Sergeant Devery was also window gazing, and no doubt *his* car would be hidden around *that* corner.

Norton gave a little stand-by signal to Valentine, and walked along to Devery. He walked past him without speaking and stopped around the corner. In a minute or two Devery moved to the corner, so that he could listen to Norton and still see anyone who might emerge from the inn.

'Is he in there?' Devery asked.

'Standing in the public bar. Dark glasses, briefcase, dark suit, dark trilby hat.'

'No pigtail?' came the dry query.

'No, but Chinese hair all right. Coarse and very black.'

'Has he seen you?'

'No doubt about that.'

'Do you think he suspects anything?'

'I shouldn't think so.'

'What about a back door to the pub?'

'A side door. He has to come out on to this street.'

'Good. Since he's seen you, you'd better go off the job. I'll put Policewoman Valentine in charge of that other car, and she'll co-operate with me. Just keep a look out while I arrange for the office to tell her.'

Devery got into his car, gave his message, and returned.

'Go back to the office and report to the D.C.I.,' he said. 'He'll find you something to do.'

'I'm sure he will,' said Norton. The sergeant could not tell whether he was pleased or displeased to be taken off the Bob Eye job. He was the most imperturbable youngest member of the C.I.D. that Devery could remember.

Chu Sen Su did not emerge from the Tudor Rose until three o'clock, and he went and stood at the bus stop near the inn. He did not appear to be intoxicated, so he obviously had not been drinking for three hours.

So it seemed that he had had a meal at the inn. It did not look like the sort of place where meals would be served regularly, so it was a reasonable assumption that Chu was known there. It would be a handy spot for him, quite close to the station from which he would catch the London train.

The bus when it arrived would pass Devery's corner, so he moved his car fifty yards back along the side street, and put it behind another parked car. He sat in his car until the bus passed, and then he waited until he saw Valentine's car go by. He followed a hundred yards behind Valentine.

Chu alighted from the bus at the terminus in Somerset Square, and he walked straight across to the Felucca Café as if that were where he had intended to go. He was not carrying his briefcase, so he must have left it at the Tudor Rose. His manner was so much lacking in furtiveness that Devery began to have doubts. Was this really Chu Sen Su? And if so, was he engaged on nefarious business?

If the answer to those questions was not negative, then the one good eye behind his dark glasses would be very busy indeed. Devery did not risk going near the Felucca, neither did the two policewomen. It would be wiser, he thought, to be content with noting and reporting movements until a more elaborate system of observations had been arranged. But distantly Chu could be seen sitting at a table in the café. Nobody but the waiter approached him. He did not seem to do any business in there.

But Chu spent time in no fewer than seven cafés or snack bars between three-thirty and half-past five. Devery thought that he must have a tremendous thirst, or else he was taking orders for China tea, or else he

161

was what he was suspected of being, a purveyor of dangerous drugs or some other undesirable commodity.

At half-past five the pubs opened, and Chu at once disappeared into the Standard of Freedom. From the Standard of Freedom he moved to the New Inn. From there he went to the Blackthorn Inn, a slightly better-class establishment. His stay at the Blackthorn was so brief that it seemed as if he had been told to depart as soon as he showed his face.

'Ah, that's better,' said Devery to himself.

When Chu moved on to the Green Archer, Devery entered the Blackthorn. The bar was empty of customers, because it was early yet. The barman was arranging tiny dishes of potato crisps on the bar.

'Hello, George,' said Devery.

'Hello, Mr. Devery.'

'I thought I saw a Chinaman come in here.'

'Happen you did. And if you'd been watching you'd have seen him go out.'

'Are you practising racial discrimination?'

'I am not. Any honest man is welcome in here, provided he's clean. But that Chinee is barred here.'

'What for?'

'Mr. Burns give me the order. He said: "If that Chinee comes in here again, his feet don't touch the floor. If he argues, bounce him." '

'Yes. But why?'

George was silent, and then he said: 'This is a respectable establishment. We don't have any funny business.'

'What sort of funny business? It's not you I'm chasing, George. It's that Chinaman. He seems suspicious.'

'Well, that's your answer. You can see he must be

getting on for fifty, but he hangs round the young stuff. Confidential talk, with the lads and lasses only just old enough to come in here. Mr. Burns don't like it, and neither do I.'

'Did you get the impression he was flogging something?'

'I thought he might be, but I never saw anything handed over. He'd do that in the toilet, happen. With the lads, at any rate.'

'I see. Thanks, George.'

Devery departed, and picked up the trail again outside a public house not far away. Chu Sen Su was apparently in the pub, and the two policewomen were watching it. The sergeant used his radio to get through to Martineau at Headquarters.

'Well?' Martineau asked.

'Our Chinese friend is running round the pubs. Earlier it was cafés. I found out he's barred at the Blackthorn. They don't like him hanging round the kids. But George the barman says he never saw anything passed. He might merely be taking orders, for delivery in a more convenient place.'

'Next time he stops at a half-way decent pub, send one of the girls in after him. And then at another pub send in the other one. Then try having a look yourself. See what he does.'

This order was obeyed. P.W. Valentine spent fifteen minutes in the same bar as Chu. It was a good-class hotel called the Stag's Head. While Devery watched the place he saw Caroline Falcon emerge. She got into her car in the forecourt, but did not immediately drive away. A minute later Chu emerged, and walked away along the street. Then Valentine came and reported.

'He was talking to a blonde girl who looked as if

163

she knew where her next fur coat was coming from. But there was the width of a table between them all the time. He didn't pass her anything, either under the table or over it.'

'Did they seem friendly?'

'He did. But I thought she was definitely stand-offish. She got up and left him.'

'Is that the girl, there? Sitting in that Triumph.'

Valentine looked. 'That's the one.'

Devery nodded, and puzzled Valentine by saying: 'I'd heard she'd reformed.'

'What's she waiting for?'

'She isn't. Look. She's going back into the Stag now that our Chinese friend is out of the way. Ah. And here is the bloke she *was* waiting for.'

They saw Leo Deluce drive up and follow Caroline into the hotel.

'Ah well,' said Devery. 'Let's get going after Who Flung Dung.'

At seven o'clock Chu Sen Su returned to the Tudor Rose, which might have been his headquarters in Granchester. The sum of observations upon him had assured the police that he had been definitely touting for something, but that he had given nothing and received nothing. The majority opinion was that he had been soliciting trade, taking orders for whatever he was selling.

Said Martineau: 'I'll make a little bet that when we search him we'll find nothing on his person. But he might have something in his briefcase.'

Said Clay: 'Don't waste any more time on him. Get him done.'

So the Tudor Rose was raided at a quarter past

eight. Upstairs, in the landlord's living quarters, Chu Sen Su was just rising from the dinner table. The landlord was indignant about the raid, and so was the landlady, and so, for a little time, was Chu. But the contents of Chu's quite bulging briefcase dispersed all indignation. There were two dozen cakes of cannabis resin, and a dozen neat little bottles of what looked like saccharine, though they were labelled 'diacetylmorphine'. Martineau said that that was another name for heroin. The illicit-market value of the drugs was estimated in thousands of pounds. Chu Sen Su was a very sad Chinaman when they took him away to lock him up.

Certain critical senior officers of the force said that the Chu case had not been properly followed up. They said that careful observations might have shown the way to *his* suppliers. Chief Superintendent Clay drily answered that further observations might have shown the way to damn all. A man who sold heroin to hapless addicts had been stopped in his career, and it would be some time before he resumed it. And when he did resume the traffic, he would stay far enough away from Clay's bailiwick.

Martineau was pleased by Devery's information about Caroline Falcon's meeting with Chu. 'Obviously she didn't want to have anything to do with him,' he said. 'She's off the stuff, as Leo Deluce said. She's been the wayward one of that pair all the time. Deluce took those three reefers off her, and when he was caught with 'em he carried the can for her. He doesn't seem to be a bad sort of lad.'

'A proper gent, in fact,' said Devery solemnly. 'Once a gentleman, always a bloody toff.'

20

Through his superior, Clay, Martineau sought and obtained permission for Sir Peter Falcon to have a police dog as an escort. The idea was put to Peter, and his mother's fears for him were stressed. He agreed to have the dog, and he also agreed to go home earlier at night, so that he could pass the dog over to his handler at the gate of Kingsmead Hall.

He and Martineau went to see Sergeant Hildred. 'Which dog will you let him have?' Martineau asked.

Hildred was just a little bit officious, as he was in any matter connected with the dogs. He answered: 'We'll have to see if one of 'em will take to him. This isn't a simple matter, you know.'

The dogs were paraded, ten of them. They were handsome animals, Alsatians every one. All of them were intelligent and well trained, but the difficulty at which Hildred had hinted became obvious. They had no friends but policemen in uniform. Everyone else was a possible enemy.

Peter was first introduced to the youngest dog, Captain.

'Good boy, Captain,' his handler said. 'This is a friend. You're to go with him.'

Captain eyed Peter warily. He did not show any hostility, nor did he wag his tail. The handler put him on a lead, and handed it to Peter. 'Go on,' he said. 'Go with him. It's your job to guard him.'

Captain moved at once. He went round Peter, until he was between him and the gate of the police station yard. He sat down.

'Come on, Captain,' Peter said, and took a step towards his car. Captain was on his feet at once, growling most ominously. His yellowish eyes were filled with a hateful threat.

'You did that wrong,' said Hildred irritably to the handler. 'You shouldn't have said aught about guarding. Now he thinks he's got to keep the gentleman here. Take him away and we'll try another dog.'

From the youngest dog Hildred went to the oldest, Saracen. 'He's got more sense than all t'others put together. He's the least friendly, but we might make him understand. Now then, Sarry, old boy, this here's a friend. Now you will be nice to him.'

Saracen understood. With Hildred holding his collar, he was allowed to smell at Peter's hand. Then, very deliberately, Peter scratched the dog's head. There was no doubt that Saracen understood but he looked extremely unhappy. Perhaps, Peter thought, he was clever enough to get the impression that he was being sold.

'He doesn't want to come with me,' he objected.

'No proper dog would want to go with a stranger,' Hildred replied. 'But he knows he's got to go, and he'll do his duty. Here, see if he'll let you put the lead on him.'

Saracen submitted to the leash with as much enthusiasm as if it were a hangman's rope.

'Come on, Saracen,' said Peter. He walked towards his Bentley, and Saracen walked sadly beside him. He obeyed when Peter told him to get up into the car, and showed a little interest as he sat up on the seat and looked around. Peter fastened the leash to the door handle, then went round and got into the driver's seat. He and the dog looked at each other eye to eye, and there was no love in Saracen's.

Peter grinned at him. 'You'll come round, you old infidel,' he said, and started the car.

Perhaps it was the novelty of riding in an open car which made a noise like a hungry lion, but Saracen began to look less forlorn as they rode through the city. On the leash again, at Falcon Tools, he walked with Peter up to his office, and sat quietly while his new master signed letters. When Peter finally rose and picked up the leash, Saracen wagged his tail. Outside, at the car again, he jumped up into his seat without being bidden.

'You're all right, boy,' said Peter. He did not secure the leash to the door handle.

Martineau made arrangements for a policeman to be on duty all day at Kingsmead Hall, as well as the two who were there at night. Lady Falcon promised that if ever she drove alone into town she would have Rajah in the car with her. For Caroline, it was arranged that Fletcher the chauffeur would drive her to the Paraguay Club when she went to meet Leo Deluce, and that Leo or one of his friends would bring her home. Leo, having been told of Peter's experience with Manuel Dominguez, also made a practice of keeping a tyre lever at hand in his car.

The precautions did not only extend to the Falcon family. Peter had a talk with Salvador Segura about possible danger to Conchita. Salvador promised that his daughter would not be left alone at the caravan, and that she would not be allowed to go out without escort. He did not think that the Manolo he had known would harm Conchita, but he remarked that trouble could change a man, and that he would take no risks.

Meanwhile Manolo was discreetly observing the people he considered to be his enemies, and he was forming remarkably accurate conclusions about them. The Falcon women were never alone, and neither was Conchita. Peter had a dog in his car. The police seemed to be coming and going much more than usual at Kingsmead. *Olé*, they were all afraid of him.

He reconnoitred the rear of the Hall grounds, and saw no policemen. But he realised that neither the wall nor the locked rear gate could be surmounted without a ladder. So he went in search of a ladder, and found one at a farm a quarter of a mile away across the fields. That is to say he saw the ladder in the distance, and doubted if he could get near to it without being challenged by the farm dog.

But haytime had started, and no doubt the farmer would soon be building a rick. He would use the ladder for that, and after the day's work was over he would leave the ladder by the unfinished rick. Manolo felt that he could afford to wait a few days, regretting that he could not risk offering his services as a hay-maker. The farm was a little too near to Kingsmead for that.

The weather remained fine, and in a day or two the farmer began to stack his hay, and then Manolo perceived the purpose of the open, roofed structure near the farmyard. He had never seen a Dutch barn before. Very convenient, he thought. The hay could be piled up there under the roof, and it would not get wet in winter.

The hay in the Dutch barn grew higher, and the ladder came into use. But the haymakers worked from dawn to dusk to make the most of the dry weather, and for his purposes Manolo wanted the ladder in daylight.

He hoped it would rain, to stop the haymaking, but it remained fine.

Every day he watched, and then one afternoon he was surprised to see the haymakers putting on their coats at five o'clock. Then he realised that it was Saturday. An evening off for the men to spend some of their wages, and drink their pints of beer. Soon all was quiet beside the Dutch barn, and the ladder was still there.

Manolo moved along the hedgerows until he was looking across a mown meadow at the ladder, and the Dutch barn was between him and the farmhouse. He crawled through the hedge which concealed him, and went and got the ladder. He carried it to the hedge, crawled through again, and dragged the ladder through. Then, taking great care and following the hedgerows, he carried the ladder the few hundred yards to the rear wall of Kingsmead Hall grounds.

From the top of the ladder he looked over the wall. He saw only woodland, a part of the garden where the grass was allowed to grow under the trees, and where daffodils and other flowers had been 'naturalised'. He mounted the wall and pulled up the ladder, and when he was down on the other side he laid the ladder on the ground. He felt sure it would not be noticed there until he had accomplished his self-appointed mission.

The woodland within the grounds covered less than an acre. From cover at the fringe of it Manolo saw horses in a paddock. Also there were tennis courts, one hard, one grass. Beyond the paddock was the rear of the stable-garage building, and continuing the same building line were greenhouses and a potting shed. Manolo's eyes narrowed as he noticed the curtained windows above the garages. Somebody lived there, then. Some servant. He watched the windows for some time, but saw no movement. Nevertheless, he moved away, right to the further edge of the one-acre wood, and made his way along the further wall until he could move along behind the greenhouses without being seen from a window.

He passed behind the garage and round to the front, taking great care at every corner. The backyard was deserted, the dog was not chained to its kennel and there was no movement behind the rear windows of the house. There was only one car in the garage. It was a Rolls-Royce, the one that he had driven on the night of his fight with the hated Englishman who had stolen his girl. It was not locked and the ignition key was in place. Manolo got into the car and lit a cigarette. He had enough cigarettes. He would wait there until his enemy came riding home in his old sports car. If anyone came in the meantime, he would lie down on the floor of the car. Tonight he would make an end of Conchita's lover. That *caballero* would be dead before he knew what had hit him.

Manolo waited as the shadows lengthened in the backyard. Occasionally he saw a woman's face at the kitchen window. He did not expect to be seen, sitting in the back of a car in the garage. About eight o'clock the back door was opened and someone let the dog out. Manolo ducked out of sight at once. The dog had been friendly one night, when Manolo had carried an exciting odour. Now, he would be different.

Manolo lay on the back seat of the car for half an hour, presuming that quite soon the dog would be taken indoors again. He heard a woman's voice calling 'Rajah, Rajah,' then again and again, and then some scolding remark in English, and then he thought he heard a door close. Good, the dog had now been taken into the house.

He sat up, and was surprised to see the dog sitting in the middle of the backyard, looking directly at him. Its steady regard convinced him that it had known he was in the car. How? Of course it had been sniffing round in the garage, and its nose had given warning of the presence of a stranger.

Manolo and Rajah considered each other, and were doing so when the house door opened again. A stout, elderly man emerged, and Manolo guessed that he was some sort of superior servant. He was not coming for the car, because he was not wearing a hat. Therefore he was coming for the dog, and all might yet be well.

The man called to the dog, and the dog ignored him. He walked to the dog and sought to grasp its collar, but the dog sidestepped deftly and easily. After several attempts to catch the dog, the man turned and stared at the garage, but Manolo was out of sight.

Crouching on the floor of the car now, with one window open a little, Manolo heard the man approach the garage. Knife in hand, he waited tensely. The man walked round the car, and probably he assured himself that no one was sitting there, but he did not come close enough to see Manolo curled up on the floor. At least, he did not *seem* to see Manolo.

Manolo heard him walk away, and saw him go back into the house. The dog resumed his sentry duty, but now Manolo was watching the windows of the house. A girl, a kitchenmaid apparently, appeared at a ground-floor window. She stared directly at the garage, and she was obviously excited. Very soon she was joined by another girl, who also stared. Then came an older woman, a stout person who was probably the cook. In a little while the cook went away, but the two girls remained. Manolo knew then that the fat man had seen enough to be suspicious. He would be telephoning for the police.

Manolo looked at the dog. Stealthily he opened the rear door of the car, holding it while he reached to open the front door. He pushed open both doors at once, and leaped out of the car. He did not have time to look at the dog, but he fell back into the driver's seat and closed the door just in time to avoid being seized by the leg.

The dog was up at the driver's window then, snarling. Manolo's answering grin was in the nature of a snarl, too. He would have loved to kill that animal.

Movement in the backyard caught his eye, and he saw that a policeman in uniform had emerged from the house, and he was striding purposefully towards the garage. Behind him walked the elderly servant, and he was carrying a poker. Manolo recognised the P.C. as the one who had arrested him the night they had taken his slumber thumb.

Manolo locked all four doors of the car and secured all the windows. He started the engine, and drove out of the garage. The policeman signalled him to stop, while the older man turned tail and ran back to the house. Manolo did not stop, but swerved towards the corner leading to the front of the house. As the car passed him, the policeman lunged to catch a door handle. He ran a few steps with the car, but had to let go.

As Manolo drove along the side of the house, heading for the front gate, he thought briefly about the dog. He looked out of the side window and saw that it was still with him, running beside the driver's door.

That meant that there would be no chance to get out and open the gate, unless he wanted to fight this huge creature with only a knife.

Distantly in the rear-view mirror he saw the police-man running after him down the drive. He slowed and drove at the gate at about ten miles an hour. There was a crack of snapping metal, and the gate flew open. He drove through, and headed down the main drive to-wards the village. In the mirror he saw the dog racing after him.

Another car appeared, coming through the stone archway from the village. It was Lady Falcon's Rolls. The person driving it must have been able to see the dog, and the running policeman had now come into sight. This driver stopped his car, and then he reversed into the archway, and stopped right in the middle of it, leaving no room for Manolo's car to pass.

For a few seconds he drove on, considering his chances of scraping through, then he turned off the drive and went back over grass, towards the field gate which was near to the gateway through which he had just passed. The dog also took to the grass, and having a shorter distance to travel it drew near to the car. Manolo swerved to run it down, but it avoided him. He turned in a tight circle, determined to kill it. The dog had ruined his plan, and it might yet bring about his capture.

Rajah seemed to know the purpose of the manœuvre. He made for the big beech tree, and reached it in time. Manolo turned away and headed for the field gate. He still had a chance to escape, by breaking down two wooden gates and reaching the road where it passed through Kingsmead Wood.

The first gate flew open as soon as the Rolls struck

it. Manolo rode bouncing across the pasture beyond, wishing that he dared drive faster on that surface. He hit the second gate and broke it down, and he was then in the little sandy lane which led to the road. Here with trees on both sides, there was no room for two cars to pass, and standing right in his way was Caroline Falcon's sports car with two people in it. Perhaps they had been making love, but they had heard the crash of the breaking gate and now he could see their startled faces.

Manolo had an idea that he might be able to push the little car out of his way. That plan was ruined by a further obstruction. Lady Falcon's Rolls appeared at the junction of the lane and the road. There was no way out.

The fugitive drove as far as he could. There was as yet no sign of the dog. He left the Rolls and approached the two in the sports car.

'*Salida*,' he said, showing his knife and making a gesture.

'Do as he says, darling,' said Caroline Falcon to Leo Deluce. 'I don't want you to get knifed.'

The two stepped out of the car. Manolo took the driver's seat and drove in reverse towards Lady Falcon's Rolls. His intention was to gain possession of the Rolls by menaces, but as he stopped near the car the dog reappeared, having found the other Rolls to be unoccupied.

In a low-slung open car Manolo felt terribly vulnerable. He knew that the relentless hound would be on him in just a few seconds. He scrambled out of the car and ran to the Rolls, demanding entrance in Spanish. But his knife was in his hand, and Lady Falcon only stared at him in terror. Her chauffeur, Fletcher, made no move to open a door.

Manolo had to turn to face the dog. It stopped, facing him, with bared teeth and glaring eyes. It kept him there, unable to move. Perhaps it had been taught to be wary of knives. Or perhaps, now that it was no longer on the premises it was supposed to guard, it remembered its early training by a man who trained police dogs. It looked dangerous enough to put Manolo in terror, but it did not attack.

Leo Deluce came running up, with a tyre lever in his hand. Seeing him, the chauffeur slipped out of the Rolls on the blind side, and came round to join him.

'Put away your knife, mate,' Deluce said.

Manolo's glance flicked towards him. He made a small gesture with the knife. Rajah's growl became a roar and he seemed about to spring. Manolo remained still.

They stood like that for some minutes, the nature of their situation hidden by the Rolls-Royce from the Saturday-night traffic which passed along the road. People in search of pleasure wondered if there had been some sort of an accident, but no vehicle stopped. They were standing like that when P.C. Baines came trotting along the sandy lane, out of breath and a little weary, but ready for action.

Baines was delighted to see Manolo. His active dealings with the Dog Man were going to finish where they had begun, and he was going to make the arrest. As they say in the police, promotion was staring him in the face.

'Well, bless us all,' he said heartily. 'It's my old dummy pal. Rolls-Royces an' all. Getting into society, aren't you, Dummy?'

He took in the situation, wondering if Rajah would recognise him as an ally. He had his doubts about that.

'Get hold of your dog,' he said to Fletcher.

With his eye on the knife, Fletcher edged forward and took Rajah by the collar. He pulled the snarling creature back, and Baines moved forward. In the changed situation Manolo turned on the only armed person he could see, Deluce who held the tyre lever. From a point of vantage twenty yards away Caroline Falcon screamed.

But P.C. Baines had something up his sleeve. It was his 'staff', the short, hard, heavy club which non-police persons refer to as a truncheon or baton. He allowed the staff to slip down into his right hand. While Manolo manœuvred to lunge at Deluce, Baines made no bones about hitting him on the head with the staff. Since policemen are usually strong men, such blows on the head are frowned upon by police authorities because they are likely to cause depressed fractures of the skull. Baines stated afterwards that he had aimed at the right shoulder, and that the target had moved.

Manolo did not suffer a fracture of the skull, but he was no more trouble after being hit. He was disarmed and handcuffed with his hands behind his back—again, against regulations—and put into the Rolls-Royce which he had stolen and damaged.

'Police Headquarters,' said Baines to Fletcher.

Lady Falcon drove herself home in her own car, with Rajah riding alert beside her. With Rajah, she felt perfectly safe.

21

There was no problem about holding Manolo in custody prior to interrogation. Two charges of taking a motor-car were undeniable, and a previous one would not be difficult to prove. There was also likely to be a charge of attempted murder, since the young Spaniard had waylaid and fought Peter Falcon with that crime in mind. He was left to meditate in a cell until Sunday morning, when Martineau would question him.

The chief inspector was in no doubt about the importance of the interrogation. The direct evidence was thin, both on the Dog Man jobs and the Falcon murder. It seemed to him that unless Manuel Dominguez could be made to talk himself into trouble, there would be no charge of murder.

He phoned the Registrar of Granchester University and asked the name of a Spanish language tutor. He was given the name and address of a Spaniard, Francisco Saumarez, who could be reached by telephone. Señor Saumarez agreed to come down to Headquarters and act as interpreter. He said: 'I'll be glad to be of help to a fellow countryman.'

'You'll be neutral, of course,' Martineau replied.

'Oh, certainly. He is from whereabouts in Spain?'

'From Barcelona. But I don't know where originally. I think he's a gypsy. You will realise that I might have to accuse him of a crime that will shock you.'

'Some Spanish gypsies are thieves.'

'This is thievery, and there may be a charge of murder.'

'I will be with you in an hour.'

That was at ten o'clock in the morning, and Señor Saumarez arrived at eleven. He was about thirty-five years of age, tall, black-haired and handsome; a Castilian from Valladolid who looked and spoke like a gentleman. Martineau liked him on sight.

Manolo had been taken to the Interrogation Room, a windowless, sound-proofed place with walls, roof, and floor of bare grey concrete. The inquisitors found him seated at a central table under a powerful overhead light. The things found in his pockets were on the table in front of him. Seated near the door were P.C. Baines and Detective Sergeant Errol. At a small table in the corner sat a C.I.D. clerk with a tape recorder and an open notebook.

Martineau introduced Saumarez to the prisoner. Manolo merely nodded, and did not offer to shake hands. He and Martineau sat facing each other, and the interpreter sat at the side, more or less between them.

'First of all,' Martineau said. 'Full name, birthplace, occupation, nationality, age, etc.'

The interpreter spoke in Spanish, and Manolo answered at some length in the same language.

'His name is Manuel Dominguez Guiterrez,' Saumarez translated. 'That is his full legal name. It means that his father's name was Dominguez and his mother's Guiterrez. In normal practice the mother's name is not used. He is twenty-five years old, and unmarried. He is a waiter by profession, and he is a gypsy. He was born near Coin in the province of Malaga, and of course his nationality is Spanish.'

Martineau nodded. He looked at the personal property on the table: a wrist-watch which was Swiss made and probably bought in England, a wad of notes which totalled £605, some loose change, a coloured handkerchief, a packet of Gauloise cigarettes, a Ronson lighter, a pair of gloves, a glass-cutter, a flashlight and a sheath knife of the double-edged sort which is sold to Boy Scouts. He moved the gloves, flashlight, glass-cutter and knife to one side, and from his pocket he took a small cellophane-wrapped packet, which he opened to show the withered 'slumber thumb'.

'This was taken from your pocket as well, you may remember,' he said as he placed it beside the knife. 'Did you carry these things when you were breaking into houses in this city?'

Saumarez translated. Manolo merely shrugged.

Martineau remembered something. He said to Baines: 'Was this man properly cautioned?'

'Yes, sir,' said Baines. 'I cautioned him soon after his arrest. I don't know if he understood.'

So Martineau said to Manolo: 'You are not obliged to answer my questions, but anything you do say will be taken down in writing and may be given in evidence.'

Manolo listened to the translation, and he did not even shrug.

Martineau picked up the slumber thumb. 'Why did you carry this if you are not a thief?'

Saumarez translated, and received an answer. He looked surprised, and then contemptuous. He said to Martineau: 'He says it is the thumb of the holy St. James.'

Martineau saw the reason for his contempt. He thought of the great shrine of Santiago de Compostella, the shrine of the saint whom the Spaniards claimed as their patron. Manolo's answer was of course a lie, but the educated Spaniard's scorn arose from the abysmal ignorance which had prompted such a lie.

Martineau picked up the grisly object. He said:

'This is called a slumber thumb. It is part of a gypsy superstition. You or your father or your grandfather took it from a corpse nine weeks in the grave, and dug up under a new moon. Under this superstition, the thief who carries the thumb believes that it prevents people from waking up while he is robbing a house. You believe that, don't you?'

Manolo listened to the translation, and shook his head. His right hand was on the table, and Martineau reached to push back the sleeve of his donkey jacket. On his wrist a tiny scar was still faintly discernible.

'And that is where you scratched your wrist when you were breaking into Kingsmead Hall, the night that Sir Richard Falcon was murdered.'

Again Manolo's answer was a shake of the head, but his expression had subtly changed. Apparently the mention of murder made him uneasy. He spoke briefly in Spanish.

Señor Saumarez said: 'He wants to know how you think he scratched his wrist.'

Martineau explained. Manolo listened to the translation, and again spoke.

Saumarez said: 'He wants to know if you think he did the murder.'

Martineau replied: 'I think he did it, and it is my aim to prove that he did.'

Manolo heard the translation of that, and sat in thought. He was definitely worried. Normally in those circumstances Martineau would have pressed him with questions to increase his harassment, but an intuitive feeling born of experience warned him to remain silent. Manolo sat and worried, and eventually he spoke to Saumarez.

Said the interpreter: 'He says the murderer was a

boy about seventeen. He has since seen the boy working in the garden at Kingsmead Hall.'

The gardener's boy! Martineau could not conceal
his astonishment. That harmless-looking lad? Well, he
had seen more unlikely murderers. He said: 'How do
you know?'

Manolo's answer was as brief: 'I was there.'

So the interrogation which Martineau had expected
to be long and difficult turned out to be short and
easy, Señor Saumarez extracted the whole story from
his compatriot. Manolo explained why the Kingsmead
watchdog did not attack him. He told how he entered
the house by a ground-floor window. He had looked
around in the hall and started to go upstairs when he
saw a moving light along the passage which led to the
rear part of the house. The light was coming towards
him, so he crept up to the top of the stairs and lay flat
there, looking down.

He saw the stranger enter the hall and look around
precisely as he had done, opening table drawers and
closing them in disappointment. He moved out into
the lobby beside the front door, and began to inspect
the contents of a cupboard there, which made Manolo
decide that he was a very inexperienced thief.

While he was searching the cupboard there was a
noise at the front door, the sound of a key in the lock.
A second later the lobby was flooded with light, and
the startled intruder hastily dodged into the recess
behind the inner door, and tried to make himself
small in there.

There was a man's voice heard briefly—Sir Richard
speaking to the dog—and then the front door was
closed and locked. Sir Richard came through the inner
door. He saw the open door of the cupboard, and

frowned. He took off his hat and white evening scarf, and was hanging them in the cupboard when he saw the youth in the recess. He approached the youth and spoke to him sternly. The youth made a faltering reply which could have been a question. Sir Richard spoke again, even more sternly. The youth produced a knife. Sir Richard spoke to him then in bitter contempt, without fear. The youth stabbed him, stooped to take his keys from his hand, and departed by way of the front door. Manolo came down the stairs. One glance at Sir Richard's wound assured him that murder had been done. He found that the front door had been left unlocked, and he also went out that way.

'Thank you, Mr. Saumarez,' said Martineau. 'The clerk will type up the statement and you can read it through and make any corrections you wish, and then sign it. I think then you can perhaps turn it back into Spanish and let the prisoner read it, if he *can* read. There will be a fee, of course.'

'Of course,' Saumarez agreed. 'I'll do the Spanish part this afternoon, if I may.'

'In a day or two, when we've got this murder sorted out, I shall want to question Dominguez about other break-ins. Will you help?'

'Only too pleased.'

22

Martineau felt that there was a need to postpone the interview with the gardener's boy until Monday. On a fine Sunday afternoon he would be out somewhere, with his friends or with a girl. He would have to be inquired for, and found. The conditions for picking him up would not be right. If he happened to be innocent, his parents would be caused unnecessary alarm. If he were guilty he might have the undeserved support of friends. The time to approach him was Monday morning, while he was working in the garden at Kingsmead Hall.

The morning of Monday was perfect, sunshine and a gentle breeze. Martineau drove to Westholme to pick up Sergeant Errol, and together they went to Kingsmead. Errol strongly doubted Manolo's story. He queried: 'If it's the boy, how did he get into the house? There was no other sign of entry except at the one window where Dominguez entered.'

'The boy is familiar with the house, at least on the outside. He might have managed to leave a window unfastened, and fastened it after he entered.'

Errol looked sceptical. Martineau did not make other suggestions, because he himself was doubtful.

In the garden at Kingsmead Hall they found the boy working with Munro, the head gardener. They were putting in bedding plants below the terrace at the front of the house.

The two detectives strolled in their direction and stood watching them. Munro looked up, and said that it was a nice morning.

'Very nice indeed,' said Martineau, with his eyes on the boy. That person was aware that he was being watched. He coloured, and appeared to give his whole attention to his work.

'What is the lad's name?' Martineau asked of Munro.

'Archie. Archie Keeler.'

'Archie,' said Martineau clearly. 'Stop work and stand up.'

Archie obeyed, and stood there trowel in hand.

'Archie,' said Martineau, very clearly now. 'I am making inquiries into the murder of Sir Richard Falcon.'

The boy stared at him speechlessly.

'Archie,' he went on. 'You were seen in the house at the time of the murder. I mean, inside the house.'

Archie dropped the trowel and ran. Errol took off after him. Errol seemed to be the faster runner, so the others stood and watched the chase. The sergeant caught the boy some two hundred yards away. There was no struggle. They began to walk back.

'You think the boy did it?' asked Munro in astonishment.

'I have reason to believe he did. What sort of a knife does he have?'

'He's using one of mine. He lost his own.'

'When did he lose it?'

'Now you mention it, it was about the time of the murder.'

'What was it like?'

'His own? He fancied himself with a sheath knife. One of those Boy Scout knives.'

'Is he afraid of Rajah?'

'No. He likes Rajah. Rajah wouldn't molest him if he came here at night.'

'I see. Thank you.'

Archie and Errol arrived. Martineau cautioned the boy, then asked: 'Why did you run away?'

'I was scared. I lost my head.'

The chief inspector's voice was quiet, not harsh at

all. 'You *were* in the house on the night of the murder, weren't you?'

The boy nodded glumly. Martineau said: 'Answer yes or no, Archie.'

'Yes.' A pause. 'Who saw me?'

'A man who was there. He saw Sir Richard catch you there. What did he say to you?'

'He was right mad. He said he was going to sack me. Then he said he'd tell the police.'

'So what did you do?'

'I got out my knife, 'cos I was frightened. He said I'd be sent away for that. Then—I don't remember.'

'I think you do.'

'Something came over me, I was that scared. I—I lost my head.'

'Did you stab him?'

Archie hung his head. Martineau said: 'Answer me yes or no. Did you stab him?'

'Yes,' said Archie.

'How did you get into the house?'

Archie looked guiltily at Munro, who was regarding him sternly.

Said Munro: 'The key of the big greenhouse fits the back door of the house. We all know that.'

'Did you use that key to get into the house, Archie?'

The boy nodded, and then managed to say: 'Yes.'

'What did you do with your knife?'

'I threw it away in Kingsmead Wood.'

'How did you get back into your own home without waking your parents?'

'On to the scullery roof and in at my bedroom window. I came out that way, an' all.'

'I see. Well, I'm afraid I shall have to take you to the police station.'

Archie nodded. 'I'm glad it's all over. It's been ter-
rible. I don't know what made me do it.'

In the presence of Señor Saumarez, Manuel
Dominguez was shown articles of jewelry which had
been stolen from various houses. Through Saumarez
he was made to understand that it would be better for
him if all his robberies were taken into consideration
at the time of his trial for the Kingsmead Hall break-
in. There would be no chance then that he might be
charged with one of the robberies at a later date. He
saw the advantage of that, and agreed to every one of
his break-ins in Granchester.

The charge of attempted murder was dropped,
mainly because Peter Falcon was against it. 'It was
very nearly a fair fight,' he said. 'And after all he did
not kill my father.'

Which showed that Peter had a sort of respect for
Manolo. It was the timeless respect which knows
neither race nor creed nor class nor colour. Manolo
was a thief because he had been raised to thievery,
but his courage and audacity were his own. Courage
is the international currency which never fails to buy
a certain esteem from men of Peter Falcon's type.

That was Manolo, but Archie Keeler was a wrong-
doer of an entirely different sort. There could have
been a certain sympathy for him because he was a
panic-stricken boy. But he had committed a burglary
not from hunger, and not having been bred in a tradi-
tion of larceny. His motive had been sheer greed, and
he had murdered a good man through selfish fear.

Archie was taken into Kingsmead Wood and he
showed the police the place where he had thrown away
his knife. The knife was found. At Police Headquarters

Archie read through his own statement and signed it in a childish hand. Though a big, well-grown youth he was still only sixteen years old. It seemed likely that he would be detained 'at Her Majesty's pleasure'. If he behaved himself he would be a free man in six, seven, or eight years. But Sir Richard Falcon would never more be seen on earth.

Sitting in the back seat of a Rolls-Royce, Conchita Segura remarked that Manolo might still be in a vengeful mood when he came out of prison.

'That doesn't matter,' said Peter Falcon. 'When he's done his time he'll be deported to Spain.'

Conchita reflected that she also might be in Spain at that time. The Segura family was about to move to London. A good contract with a London theatre company had been signed. Fame beckoned, but both Salvador and Pepe had been showing signs of nostalgia. Spain also beckoned. Conchita knew that they would return, but as famous people. What would happen if poor Manolo sought them out there? Salvador would brush him aside. There would be trouble and the police would come. Poor Manolo, her childhood sweetheart. Conchita toyed with a diamond bracelet which Peter had given her, and for a minute or two she felt rather sad.

›› If you've enjoyed this book and would like to discover more great vintage crime and thriller titles, as well as the most exciting crime and thriller authors writing today, visit: ››

The Murder Room
Where Criminal Minds Meet

themurderroom.com

www.ingramcontent.com/pod-product-compliance
Ingram Content Group UK Ltd.
Pitfield, Milton Keynes, MK11 3LW, UK
UKHW040436280225
455666UK00003B/99